Leaf of Faith

Isabella Proctor Cozy
Mysteries
Book 1

Lisa Bouchard

For Paul, who supports all my crazy dreams.

Table of Contents

Chapter 1

Being a witch wasn't something we talked about with customers. It's been over four hundred years since my ancestor Elizabeth Proctor was convicted of witchcraft, and the fear of being found out still ran deep. That was why, on the surface, the witches in Portsmouth seemed like normal people. Okay, maybe not normal. Maybe harmlessly eccentric.

Take me, for example: I looked like any other twenty-one-year-old shopgirl with two jobs trying to make it on her own. I was five foot seven, and had black hair, dark blue eyes, and features that, to me, seemed too large for my face. My best friend, Abby, said I was glamorous, but I thought I was more of an ugly duckling. Abby has always been the beautiful one, with delicate features, gleaming golden hair, and the kind of grace and physical presence that resulted from over a decade of dance classes.

Maybe I wouldn't have stood out in a crowd, but I was one of the few potion witches in New Hampshire.

I grasped the ornate brass doorknob and pushed open the door to the Portsmouth Apothecary. The shop always smelled like the tea of the day, and today's was rose hip and hibiscus. I closed the door behind me and took a moment to survey the sales floor. The jars of herbs that lined the right-hand side of the shop were running low despite the stock we kept in the prep room, the candle display in the center of the room needed to be refilled, and several of the touristy knickknacks in front of the large picture window had been knocked off the table.

I quickly made my way to the office in the back where I hung up my coat and pulled my hair back into a bun. I loved this store and using my talents as a potion witch to help people—human and witch—even if the humans didn't realize magic was involved.

Once I returned to the main room, I looked to Trina Bassett, my boss. Her lips were pinched in frustration and her left eye twitched. She was busy helping Mrs. Williams with an order. Mrs. Williams was in her seventies, but dressed and acted at least two decades younger. She was extremely particular and would choose each bud of lavender and chamomile for her tea blend. It took ages to complete her order every week. I could tell by the way Trina was holding her short, round body rigid that she was almost at the end of her patience.

"Good morning, Isabella," Trina called to me as she pulled a jar of lavender from its spot on the shelf and showed it to Mrs. Williams.

I smiled at her, hoping she'd read my encouragement. "Morning, Trina. Morning, Mrs. Williams."

Mrs. Williams pointed a bony finger to several lavender buds and Trina delicately pulled them out with a pair of tongs. Ordinarily, we use a scoop to remove the herbs from their jars, but not for Mrs. Williams. A half pound of tea might take an hour to assemble for her.

The clouds broke and sun flooded through the front window. The light reflected off the pale yellow walls, bathing the shop in a warm glow. March in New Hampshire was almost always gray, but these moments of sunshine reminded us better weather was coming. A glint of sunlight bouncing off a shard of broken glass near the herb jars caught my eye. I wanted to ask Trina what happened today that the shop was in such disarray, but that would have to wait until Mrs.

Williams left. I grabbed the broom and dustpan from the closet by the back door. As I closed the closet door, Mrs. Williams raised her voice.

"I don't care what you think, Trina, you know the right thing to do, and I expect you to take care of it by tonight. I won't be held responsible if you don't."

Not wanting to intrude, I stood at the checkout counter in the back of the room. Once Mrs. Williams left, I swept the glass up while Trina replaced the flower jars she had been using. "What was that all about?" I asked.

"It's nothing to worry about, my dear," she said. Her grimace told me otherwise. I'd been Trina's apprentice for about a year, and she didn't hide her worry nearly as well as she thought she did.

I continued sweeping and found more shards of glass and sliced dong quai root. I picked the dong quai container off the counter to inspect it. It had been replaced by one of the new, wider jars Trina had been slowly changing to. Why had the old jar broken, and more importantly, why hadn't Trina cleaned it up completely?

Before I could ask, Trina handed me a glass vial. "Your investiture ceremony is coming up soon, right?"

"It's next week. Are you coming?"

"I wouldn't miss it for the world," Trina

said.

Investiture was the time once every seven years that a witch chose what she would focus her work and study on. My cousins Thea and Delia and I would choose our first non-beginner focus. I planned to choose potions, and I didn't know what Thea or Delia would choose.

"In that case, it's time for a test. I'll finish tidying up. You have half an hour to tell me the eight components of this potion."

I blew hair out of my face and took the vial with me to my small counter in the prep room, across from the office. The small room had two counters, two chairs, and all our extra stock on shelves that lined three sides of the room. We kept the lights dim, because we stored photosensitive ingredients there.

Unlike the sales floor, the prep room smelled green and earthy. I sat in my chair, closed my eyes, and focused my mind. There was a standard method to determine potion ingredients, and as long as I worked through all the steps in the allotted time, I should be able to pass the test. I could cast a spell to determine the ingredients, but Trina was old-fashioned and wanted me to learn the non-magical methods I could use in front of customers. The first two tests were simple: smell and sight. I unstoppered the cork and immediately smelled pungent ginger oil. I poured the potion into a bowl and recognized the glimmer of pearl powder. Was this a longevity potion?

Before I moved to the next step, Trina opened the door. "Your mother called and said she needs you to call her right away."

I was concentrating on my test and hadn't heard the phone ring. I rubbed my forehead. Anytime my mother had something she wanted to tell me, it was urgent—at least to her. I didn't want to interrupt my test for something that could wait for another twenty-five minutes.

"Did you tell her I was busy?"

"No, I didn't. Call her, and if you need a few more minutes to finish, you can have them. I'll be in the office if you need me."

I pulled my phone from my pocket and dialed. "Hi, Mom. I'm in the middle of a test. What's up?"

"Hi, sweetie, I know I said I wouldn't bother you when you moved out. It's been weeks since we've seen you, and we miss you," she said with a shaky voice.

I thought over the six months since I'd moved out and realized she was right. I'd planned on a slow withdrawal from daily family life when I moved out of the house to make the separation easier on everyone. I was the first person in two generations to move to an apartment, and my grandmother, mother, and aunts were all sad about my choice.

"Sorry about that. It's been incredibly busy and by the time I remember to call, it's too late at night."

"I need you to come to dinner tonight. I'm worried about your grandmother. Her health has taken a turn, and we can't figure out what is wrong," she said with more distress in her voice than I'd heard in a long time.

My heart sank. Grandma was seventy-seven, and although witches can live to twice that age, it wasn't guaranteed. "Sure, I can come for dinner, but how can I help?"

"Your grandmother listens to you, and I want you to convince her to see a doctor. Can you ask Trina to come by and have a look at her too?"

Grandma was stubbornly independent, thinking she knew enough herbal magic to keep herself alive almost forever. She started listening to my advice only once I'd become Trina's apprentice.

"I'm not sure she'll listen to me, but I'll give it a try."

"Good. Dinner is at six. Don't be late."

I hung up and turned to my potion, trying to put my worry about Grandma out of my mind.

"Is everything okay?" Trina asked from the doorway.

I looked up at her, willing myself to not

cry. "Grandma's not well, and my mother and aunts can't figure out what's wrong. They want me to convince her to go see a doctor."

Trina shook her head. "Your grandmother's never seen a doctor in her life, I doubt she'll start going to one now."

"Can you come talk to her tonight?"

"I can't. I've got someone coming to the shop after hours. I have another idea. Leave the test vial here, and let's head out to the greenhouse."

I followed Trina out the back door and pulled my black cardigan tight against the cold March air. The rose and juniper bushes planted next to the greenhouse rustled in the wind. Our feet crunched on the gravel path that was finally devoid of snow.

The greenhouse was a small glassed-in building she had built in the shared courtyard behind the apothecary that provided most of the herbs and flowers we needed. The floor-to-ceiling shelves were full of rare and common plants we used in our tinctures, sold as dried goods, or ground into powder. I stepped in and took a deep breath. The oxygen-rich air, heady with the scent of early blooming roses and echinacea, cheered me. The bright flowers were a stark contrast to the dirty gray snow piled up along the edges of the courtyard and hinted at the change of season everyone longed for by the end of winter.

I'd learned a lot of gardening from my grandfather when I was younger, and I used his lessons to keep the greenhouse plants thriving. Grandpa and I spent our weekends year-round working on the family gardens: food, flower, memorial, and medicinal. If we weren't outside working in them during the warm months, we were by the fireplace in winter, planning changes and additions, or starting seeds in early spring.

Trina closed the door. "It's time for you to start using your powers to assemble potions. You've learned what each of these plants will do. Now you need to put that information together with what you know about other people to form an effective cure. You've been honing your intuition over the past year, and it's time to use it."

I stared at her, mouth open. "You want me to guess?"

She put her hand on my shoulder and gave it a reassuring squeeze. "No, I want you to think about someone you're close to, someone you care about, and then let your instinct guide you."

We stood silently for a moment while I thought.

"Who have you chosen?"

"Grandma," I said.

Trina smiled. "I thought you'd pick her. Use your intuition and choose tincture, tea, or balm."

"Tincture, because it will be easier to add to her food," I said.

"Be wary, giving any medical assistance to someone without their permission is the first step in harming them and yourself."

"I know." It went deeper than that. Using magic on non-magical people was almost unilaterally frowned on. Healing potions were one of the very few exceptions, but even then, the person had to know the ingredients they were buying. There was no exception when the person being treated was a witch.

"Close your eyes and focus on your grandmother. Once you have her in mind, allow your intuition to guide you to the plants she needs. Once you have identified each one, we'll go inside and you will make the tincture."

I bit my lip and closed my eyes. Once I had Grandma firmly in mind, the lemon tree, the rosemary bush, and the small juniper bush outside the greenhouse took her place in my vision. I opened my eyes. "Lemon, juniper and rosemary."

Trina nodded. "Okay then, pick a little of each and meet me inside."

When I returned to the prep room, I put the tincture ingredients on my table and looked into the office, where Trina was on her cell phone with her back to me.

Leaf of Faith

Her shoulders stiffened. "Where do you think I'm going to get that kind of money?"

A man was yelling on the other end of the line, but I didn't recognize his voice. It could have been anyone, because the phone made his voice sound tinny.

"I don't care where you get it, or what you need to do to get it. I'm coming today and you don't want to disappoint me."

Chapter 2

Trina slammed the phone on her desk without saying another word.

I knocked on the office doorframe. "You okay?"

Trina turned to me, blinking back tears. "I'm fine. Or at least I will be, once I get him sorted out."

I smiled and said okay, but I didn't believe her. Her lower lip quivered, and she forced herself to smile at me.

"Let's talk about something important. Explain why your grandmother needs these," Trina said.

"Lemon will strengthen her blood, juniper will increase her appetite, and rosemary will help clear mental fog."

"These are good for any woman her age, and if they clear up the problem, then there's nothing seriously wrong with her." She sat on the edge of her desk and sighed. "The problem is getting her to take it. Do you think she'll take it because you asked her to? Or will you have to convince her?"

"I thought I would tell her it was part of my homework, and that you approved it. She might have more faith in it then."

"Consider the best way to approach her while you prepare your ingredients. Don't worry about the test. You can finish it tomorrow."

After a half hour of potion making, I passed my hand over the filled vial and whispered my intention: "Restore Grandma's health."

Anyone could make a potion from a book, but it was the magical intention a witch added at the end of the process that gave it real potency.

I brought the potion to Trina to check. She cast a subtle spell with the flick of her finger to check my potion.

"Juniper, lemon, rosemary. Good work. Your intention is strong, too. Tell your grandmother I said she'd be foolish not to take it. She may need more than one dose, spread out over a few days, before she is well again. If she gets worse, though, stop giving it to her immediately." She handed me the vial and picked up an envelope off her desk. "Watch the shop for me while I run this to the mailbox."

I slipped the vial into my pocket. We had no customers, so I took the lavender and chamomile jars to the prep room to fill. I was halfway finished when the alarm on my phone went off. Time to leave for my second job—the one that paid my bills.

While I learned a lot from Trina, being her apprentice didn't pay. I had to work thirty hours a week at my second job, counter staff at The Fancy Tart Café. It wasn't the worst job ever, and Bethany Swift, the owner, was reasonable as far as bosses go. Someday, though, I wanted to run my own potions shop.

You might think I'd have no worries being a witch, because I could make my own luck, conjure up all the money I needed, and create love potions to attract anyone I wanted. The witchcraft my family practiced was not like that.

We followed some strict rules, because there were big consequences if you broke them. From the horror stories I heard as a kid, I knew I would never, ever use magic for personal gain, because the price was too high. You've heard the stereotype of ugly crones? Those were witches who used their power for selfish reasons.

I grabbed my coat and peered out the window. I didn't want to leave the shop until she got back, but I didn't want to be late for work either. I closed my eyes and relaxed the tension in my jaw. Trina would return any second and the café was only a couple blocks away.

The door chimes rang and I opened my eyes.

"I'm sorry, I got stuck talking to Caroline and couldn't break away. I'll see you tomorrow?" Trina said.

I smiled. Caroline Arneson would ruin anyone's day. She wanted the apothecary space to expand her own tourist shop, but Trina steadfastly refused to move.

"Yes. I'll be here before ten. Do you want me to bring coffee?"

Trina said no to coffee and reminded me once again that we never cast spells on or treat another person without permission. I agreed, but thought she sounded more like I was about to go full Darth Vader when all I wanted was to get a bit more spring in Grandma's step.

I walked the two blocks to The Fancy Tart, trying not to look in each shop window full of new spring merchandise. I loved the quaint all-brick feel of Market Street and its tourist vibe, but I didn't have time for window-shopping today. When I wasn't running late, I loved looking up at the five-story buildings that surrounded Market Square and dreaming of owning one of the condos that the upper floors housed. The variety of shops in the square practically guaranteed I'd never have to leave the area for anything I might want. I didn't have a car and wouldn't ever need one here in Portsmouth. I opened the kitchen door of the bakery and clocked in two minutes late.

I put my things in my locker and stood in front of the six-foot-tall oven that was baking rye and pumpernickel loaves. I stretched my hands out, warming them after the cold walk from the apothecary.

Bethany, my boss, turned from the papers on her desk in the corner of the kitchen and brushed a lock of curly gray hair out of her face. She had flour on her pointed nose and a grin on her wide lips. "Isabella, hi. Is it two already?"

"Yup. What do you want me to focus on today?" Some days there were special projects she wanted done, and on others I waited on customers, so I always checked first.

"We've been busy today. Start by waiting on customers."

"You got it."

I walked through the kitchen, weaving my way between the metal tables the bakers used to knead dough. It was quiet, because the three large floor mixers situated against the back wall were all off. I said hi to the afternoon baker, Andrew. Andrew was Bethany's younger brother, and at sixty-eight, he still had enough energy to put me to shame. "Hey, Isabella. How's it going?"

"Not too bad. What's good today?"

He grinned. "It's all good. The last batch of croissants are exceptionally flaky, so I suggest those."

My mouth watered in anticipation. If there were any left by the time I took a break, I'd share one with Abby.

Pushing through the saloon doors that separated the front of the store from the kitchen, I was surprised to see a line of customers snaking through the store and ending at the door. The glass-fronted bakery cases were running low on product, but what was there was arranged neatly. Students who needed their early-afternoon caffeine fix occupied all the oak tables.

I looked up at the chalkboard hanging behind the point-of-sale system to see the specials. We were out of honey lavender tea, but the cardamom rose coffee was still available.

The next person in line caught my attention. It was Chuck Mitchell, our downstairs neighbor. He usually tried to jockey position so that Abby Allen, my best friend since kindergarten, would wait on him.

"I can help you here, Chuck," I said with my brightest grin. Chuck was sort of handsome, if you liked neck beards and hair that perpetually needed to be combed. Unfortunately for Chuck, Abby preferred the athletic, clean-cut type. Her preference didn't keep Chuck from asking her out at least once a week, though.

"Hi, Belle," he said with a smirk.

Being called Belle, Bella, or anything other than my actual name bugged me to no end. He knew it, and he liked to see me cringe every time he pulled this stunt. Surprisingly, he hadn't realized that antagonizing your crush's best friend wasn't the way to win her heart.

"Not a Disney princess," I muttered, before more loudly saying, "What'll it be?"

"I'll have the usual, princess."

His "usual" was a tall hot mocha with eight creams and four sugars. Yes, that was four sugars *after* the sweetened chocolate syrup. I swore someday I was going to go into sugar overload just making this coffee. I made his drink, grabbed the worst looking chocolate chip muffin in the case, and handed him his order.

Now, when I said the worst looking muffin, I didn't mean it was bad; Bethany would have none of that. It was a bit smaller and had fewer chips than the others. Was it petty to do this? I contend it was much less petty than his continuing to call me Belle—he earned it.

I rang him up and scowled at his retreating back, because he always left a five-dollar bill in

Abby's tip jar, no matter who waited on him. As soon as he left, she plucked the bill out of her jar and put it into mine.

My next customer was another regular, although I knew hardly anything about her but her first name. Today, Agatha was dressed in a suit as though she was on a break from work, even though she had a hard time keeping a job. Her brown hair was held in a bun by two pencils, and I was pleased to see that she was wearing matching shoes. Sadly, that didn't always happen. She was arguing with Alice, the voice in her head, and as she stepped up to the counter, it seemed like she was losing the argument.

"Hi, Agatha, can I help you?"

"Two buttermilk scones and two chamomile teas. We can't afford the caffeine this late in the day."

"Right away." I pulled the scones out of the pastry case. "How are you and Alice today?"

"She wants cardamom rose coffee, but that will keep her up all night. She's arguing that I never let her have any fun."

I turned to make the two cups of tea. Agatha had been a customer at the apothecary for at least a year, and I wasn't sure anything Trina and I could come up with would help her. She most likely needed psychiatric help, but never followed up on our suggestion to call a doctor. I handed her the tea and scones. "Stop by the apothecary and talk to Trina. Maybe she'll have something new for you to try."

Before I knew it, my shift was over, and it was time for me to head to my family's house. I had been too busy serving customers to worry about Grandma, but as I walked down Market Street, I felt a sense of wrongness that I'd only ever sensed once before: the day my Great Aunt Jem was murdered.

Chapter 3

I stood in the driveway of Proctor House, my family's home, trying to determine where the feeling of dread was coming from.

As I scanned the windows of the three-story blue colonial house, nothing jumped out at me except that the white trim would need to be repainted this summer. So much for honing my intuition.

I closed my eyes and allowed my senses to roam through all the rooms in the house, trying to find anything dangerous, but I couldn't pin the feeling down. I wanted to find something to fix, something to make Grandma get well.

The aroma of Aunt Nadia's garlic-covered roast wafted out as soon as I opened the door. My mouth began to water as I greeted my family.

The kitchen was the center of the house for us. Aunt Nadia, Aunt Lily and my mother, Michelle—collectively called "the aunts" by my cousins and me—owned a catering business when we were younger, and they had expanded the kitchen to accommodate the extra work. We had an eight-burner stove, three stand mixers, and more pots, pans, and utensils than we would use in three lifetimes. We could almost always be found sitting at the kitchen table, drinking tea, laughing, helping Aunt Nadia cook, or just being together.

Tonight, the aunts and my cousins were cooking in a ballet of movements and stove use. Delia, whose blonde hair had red tips, was slicing apples. Thea, who had no time for the extended beauty routines Delia loved, had her brown hair up in a bun. She was singing *Peel Me a Grape* as she sautéed brussels sprouts.

Aunt Nadia, Delia's mother, had taken after her daughter and had colored her long blonde hair black, with the exception of one streak of white in the front. She pushed Thea out of the way and opened the oven door. "The roast will be ready in ten minutes," she said.

Aunt Lily, the most somber of us all, preferred her brown hair in a bob—no muss, no fuss, she proclaimed. She was mashing the potatoes at the kitchen table.

Leaf of Faith

My mother, the most beautiful of the aunts, at least to me, was rolling out piecrust for the apples Delia was slicing. Surprisingly little magic was used in the kitchen, because sometimes a good tool, like the rotary apple peeler, was easier to use than magic. Mashing potatoes, on the other hand, was the perfect place for Aunt Lily's smashing spell.

My mother wiped her hands on her apron. "Isabella, I didn't even hear you come in." She wrapped me in a big hug and kissed my cheek.

"Where's Grandma?" I asked.

"By the fire in the living room. She hasn't been able to get warm all day," my mother said as she picked up a steaming mug of tea. "Bring this to her for me?"

I took the mug and hoped I could talk Grandma into a couple drops of the potion I made for her.

At the entrance to the living room, smoke from the fireplace brought back memories of toasting marshmallows when we had winter power outages. The few flames in the dying fire flickered and barely lit the marble hearth. Grandma had moved her favorite red wingback chair as close to the fireplace as possible. She sat with a shawl wrapped over her hunched shoulders. She hadn't taken the time to brush her long white hair, and there was no color in her usually pink cheeks.

"Hi Grandma," I said. "I brought you some fresh tea with honey to warm you up."

She smiled at me. "It's lovely to see you, my dear. I miss you when you're not here every day. I feel like things are happening in your life and I don't know what they are anymore. I wish you would reconsider and move home." She took the mug from my hand and blew across the top of the hot drink.

I put three logs on the fire and nudged them into place with the wrought-iron poker. "I'd rather talk about you and your health."

Grandma raised an eyebrow but said nothing.

I sat on the floor at Grandma's feet, feeling the heat sink into my chilly toes. "Today Trina brought me out to the greenhouse and had me think about a person. Once I had that person firmly in mind, she had me think about all the plants in the greenhouse until some of them called to me." I paused for a moment, wondering if Grandma would laugh at how funny it sounded. When she didn't, I continued. "Some of them did, and I made you a remedy."

Grandma scoffed. "What could you possibly make me that I haven't already made for myself at one time or another? I've made pretty much everything over the course of my life, and even though I'm not as good as you are, I can get the job done."

I looked past her and studied the pattern of the room's reproduction colonial wallpaper while I gathered my thoughts. "The idea was to use my abilities to choose the right elements for you." I took the small bottle from my pocket and held it up to her. This has lemon, juniper berry, and rosemary. I made it myself, under Trina's supervision."

Grandma took the bottle. "And both you and Trina say this will be good for me?"

I nodded. "We're all worried about you. You're sitting here in the dark, wrapped up in a shawl instead of bossing everyone around in the kitchen. Something's not right."

Grandma furrowed her brow.

"This is my homework, too."

"I don't need it," she said. She set the bottle on the table by her chair, next to her tea. "Let's go see if dinner is ready."

Pushing Grandma when she said no would be a mistake. The aunts would find another chance for me to bring it up over dinner. I helped Grandma up from the chair, something I never would have had to do a few weeks ago. She grabbed my arm and we started slowly walking to the kitchen. I bit my lip to keep tears from springing to my eyes. Grandma was my rock, and after losing Grandpa last year, I wasn't ready for another death in the family.

In the dining room, Delia had lit another fire in the fireplace. The lively flames flickered and reflected off the sconces above the sideboard on the far side of the room. This was the smaller of the two dining rooms in the house, and we called it the Blue Room for its blue toile wallpaper. The cherry table sat eight, and we still left the head of the table empty in memory of Grandpa.

"Grandma, come sit here next to the fire," Delia said.

Grandma walked to the chair Delia pulled out for her. "That sounds lovely, thank you."

As I sat at the dining room table, a sense of completeness settled over me that living in my apartment didn't give. Nothing felt as good as being surrounded by family, but if I gave into this comfort and moved home, it wouldn't be long before I felt overprotected and wanted to move out again. My desire for freedom, even though being on my own was sometimes scary, outweighed my desire to live at home.

The aunts handed serving dishes around the table, and Delia made sure Grandma got some of everything on her plate, even though her eyes were beginning to close.

Thea put her hand on Grandma's shoulder and gave it a small shake. "Grandma, you need to wake up and eat dinner," she said.

Grandma snorted. "Missing a meal once in a while isn't going to kill me."

My mother's fork clanged as it fell to her plate. "Mother, how could you say that?"

"Take it easy, Michelle. You're not going to get rid of me so easy—I plan to be around for a long time to come," Grandma said.

My mother wiped tears from her eyes with her napkin.

"In fact," Grandma continued, "Isabella and Trina made me a potion that should have me feeling much better in a few days." She turned to me. "Go get the bottle and I'll have some with dinner. We can't have your mother thinking I'm going to die any day now."

I gave her a quick smile and fetched the bottle. "Three drops at first to see how it works for you."

"It's too bad Trina isn't here," my mother said.

"She had an after-hours client," I said. "She approved of the ingredients, and I've been making these tinctures long enough that she doesn't worry about my process."

"If she's sure . . ." my mother said.

Aunt Lily came to my rescue. "Give the girl a break. She's been studying for almost a year with Trina, and she's learned more than you or I will ever know. If Trina says it's okay, then it is."

Grandma put three drops in her mouth and took a drink of water. "There. Now none of you have to worry."

Grandma sat up straighter in her chair, but her eyes were still drooping with exhaustion.

At the end of the meal, Delia went into the kitchen to get the apple pie from the oven, and while she was gone, Aunt Lily sat bolt upright and moaned.

"Mom, what's wrong?" Thea asked from across the table.

"Keep your children close. It is dangerous if they stray."

Chapter 4

When Aunt Lily was done talking, her shoulders slumped and her eyes closed. It had been quite a while since Aunt Lily had been seized by a vision, and I had forgotten that she occasionally had them. The last time I saw one, I was ten years old.

"Help me to bed, girls," whispered Aunt Lily. Having a prophecy was exhausting, so we brought her upstairs and tucked her into her bed. I kissed her on the forehead and told her not to worry about anything tonight. Thea stayed with her while Delia and I left.

Back downstairs, Delia and I rejoined our mothers in the dining room.

"Where's Grandma?" Delia asked.

My mother blew her nose. "In the living

room. Isabella, there's only one thing this prophecy could mean."

I rolled my eyes. I didn't want to hear her tell me, for the millionth time, that it was unsafe for me to live anywhere except Proctor House. "I know, Mom. You think it's not safe for me to have an apartment with Abby. I can't do it, I'm not like you. I can't be happy if all I ever know is life here. I need to be on my own for a while, live my own life, make my own mistakes."

"And if those mistakes cost you your life?" she spat back.

Sure, that's what the prophecy seemed to say, but they were never straightforward, and they never seemed to mean what you first thought.

"You're being a bit overdramatic," I said.

My mother pushed her chair away from the table and stormed into the living room. Aunt Nadia followed her, trying to calm her down.

"If you called more often, she would be less upset," suggested Delia.

I blew out a sigh. "I know. And I don't imagine it's easy seeing you and Thea here every night but not me."

"It's not easy for her, but you haven't done anything wrong."

"Sure doesn't feel like it," I said.

When my mother and aunt returned to the dining room, they both had red-rimmed eyes.

Leaf of Faith

"Delia, why don't you help me put this pie away," Aunt Nadia said.

Delia smirked. We all knew it was an excuse for mom and me to have a little time alone.

"Before you say anything, I want you to know I'm not mad at you. I'm worried for you all the time. I'll try to keep that in check from now on," my mother said.

I gave her a hug. "What mother doesn't worry about her daughter? I promise I'll call more often."

I let her go and she squeezed my hand. "That would be nice. Will you stop by tomorrow and look in on Grandma?"

"Of course."

"Do you want to stay for dessert?"

I shook my head. "No thanks. I'm going to have an early night."

She walked me to the kitchen door and kissed my forehead before I left.

For a nice change, it wasn't drizzly out. The temperature had dropped, though. I walked the ten blocks down the brick sidewalks of Market Street to my apartment building. Shops were all closed, and rather than window-shop, I looked up at the half moon that lit up the night sky.

Lights in five of the six apartments in my building were on when I got there. Only the middle apartment on the first floor was dark, probably because Mr. Subramanian, my landlord, was done renovating for the day. I took the stairs to the second floor, passed Mrs. Thompson's apartment and unlocked the door to the apartment I shared with Abby. She was on the brown leather couch watching a movie with a big bowl of popcorn.

Our apartment was the perfect size for us. Two bedrooms, one bath, one galley kitchen and a living room with a small dining area. We'd covered most of the ecru carpet with brightly patterned area rugs and tried to get thrift shop furniture that didn't clash too badly.

"How was dinner?" Abby asked.

I flopped down next to her on the couch and popped a piece of popcorn in my mouth. I chewed and sighed.

"That bad?" she asked.

"It was about the same as usual. It's always nice to be there, but I hate the pressure I get at every turn to move home."

Abby laughed. "Yeah, mom guilt will get you."

"True, except I have mom guilt, aunt guilt, cousin guilt, and worst of all, grandma guilt."

"It's like an entire holiday's worth of guilt all at once," Abby laughed.

She wasn't wrong. Most families didn't all live together like ours did. Even other witch families were satisfied living close together but not in the same house. So for other families, our evening dinner felt a lot more like a holiday, because everyone was there.

I took another piece of popcorn. "Yeah, I suppose so. But what are you gonna do?" I asked.

"You're not going to give in and move home, right?"

There was no chance this was going to happen. "No way, I worked too hard to get out without hurting everyone's feelings to move back now. I've got too many plans for a life that doesn't revolve around the Proctor House."

I didn't want to keep talking about my family, so I glanced at the TV. Abby was watching the movie that always cheered her up.

"*Enola Holmes* again? What happened?" I asked.

Abby sniffled. "I asked Bethany to give me more training, and she turned me down. Again."

Poor Abby. She was desperate to make something of herself and had set her sights on running The Fancy Tart when Bethany retired. The problem was, Bethany had already hinted she wanted me to run it. I couldn't run it and be a potion witch at the same time. I just hadn't figured out a way to let Bethany know without disappointing her.

If only there was a way to get Bethany to

see how hard Abby was trying. If Bethany spent as much time training Abby as she did with me, Abby would get much better.

"The first thing you have to do is stop complaining about early mornings. If you want to move up in this job, you're going to have to embrace working at ridiculously early hours."

Abby squeezed her eyes shut. "It's bad enough I have to be in before the sun comes up, but to be happy about it?"

"You don't need a jedi mind trick to change her perception of you, just stop complaining about the early shifts," I said. "She thinks I'm great because I don't mind being up early and I don't complain about it. I don't work any harder or any better than you do, but she sees me as a better worker."

Abby sighed. "No way around it then, it's fake it until you make it time." She looked at her watch. "I guess I'm going to have to go to bed once this movie is over."

She'd be in bed by nine, and there was no way she would fall asleep before midnight, but at least she would try. And I could help a little. "Let me make you some restful night tea to help you sleep."

Abby didn't always like my tea, so she grimaced. "As long as it doesn't have bergamot in it."

I walked into the kitchen and tried the exercise Trina and I did earlier. I thought about

Leaf of Faith

Abby and her need to get to sleep. I pulled chamomile, tilia, and valerian from my small personal stock. No bergamot needed. I put the kettle on to boil and washed the last couple dishes in the sink while I waited.

What was happening with Grandma's health? During the last snowstorm she was shoveling the back stairs, because she was frustrated that our snowplow guy hadn't come yet. For her to be exhausted all the time meant something was wrong. Aunt Lily's prophecy was worrying, too.

The teakettle whistled, and I poured the hot water over the cute tea ball I'd given Abby for her birthday. In the living room, *Enola Holmes* was getting close to the end.

Abby sniffed the tea I handed her. "Thanks."

She blew across the tea before taking a sip. I wanted her to have some tea before I told her about Grandma. Abby loved my Grandma, mostly because Grandma had always been kind to her. Most witch kids started losing friends in middle school, because kids could tell when someone was different. Abby didn't care if I was different; she stood by me. This loyalty earned Abby a place in Grandma's heart forever.

"There's one other thing I wanted to tell you."

Abby looked at me and said, "Yeah?"

"Grandma's not doing well."

Abby bit her lip as she set her tea down on the coffee table. "What is it?"

"We're not sure. You know Grandma, she's not about to go see a doctor."

"Is it serious?"

I took one of her hands in mine and decided it would be best to tell her the truth. "She was fine a couple weeks ago, but now she seems to have lost all her strength. She is falling asleep at all hours of the day and can't stay warm."

Tears welled in Abby's eyes. She would be as devastated at the loss of Grandma as anyone else in my family. "I made something at the apothecary that I got her to take with her dinner, and maybe that will help."

Abby scoffed. "I know your family likes the old remedies, but what if it's something serious this time? What if it's something some tea and rest won't cure?" She jumped up off the couch and paced back and forth in our living room. "We need to make a plan. We need to get her to see a real doctor."

She sat down and couldn't control her tears anymore. "This sounds exactly like what happened to my grandpa. He started winding down, and it wasn't until after he died that we found out what was wrong with him. He had cancer and didn't tell anyone. He never had any treatment and he died."

After this, she crumpled into my arms and sobbed. I got her to drink more tea, because by the time she finished it, she wouldn't be awake for long. We relaxed on the couch and watched the last few minutes of the movie in silence.

When the credits rolled, I turned the TV off. "You look exhausted. Let's get you to sleep so you can make a good impression on Bethany tomorrow morning."

Abby looked at me through sad, bleary eyes. "You sure you'll be okay?"

I squeezed her hand. "Don't worry about me, I'll be fine. I'll visit Grandma tomorrow and I promise we'll work something out."

I hoped I hadn't just lied to my best friend.

Chapter 5

The next day I went straight to the apothecary to talk to Trina. I needed advice on how to deal with my overprotective family. When I got to the front door, a sharp chill ran through my body — the same warning I had last night at Proctor House. The door to the apothecary was unlocked. Another bad sign. The shop was in shambles. Every single jar of potions and dried herbs or other ingredients had been knocked off the shelves. The larger jars hadn't broken, but the smaller ones had, leaving a stinking puddle in the middle of the room. Candles had been swept off the top of the display, and the table of tourist items had been flipped over.

"Trina!" I yelled, but she didn't answer.

The office and prep room had also been

tossed, but Trina wasn't in either of them.

I rushed out back to the greenhouse. I opened the door and gagged on the stench of rubbing alcohol. I held my breath and searched for her quickly. She wasn't there either. Adrenaline pumping, I left the greenhouse and walked around one side of it. A patch of dark, dry blood on the ground and drag marks warned me something was wrong. I followed the marks, my heart pounding, as they led me behind the juniper bushes next to the greenhouse.

My knees went weak when I saw Trina, lying face up on the ground. *This couldn't be!*

"Oh no, no," I wailed.

I bent down to check her pulse, but there was no movement under her cold, lifeless skin. I sank to the ground, taking in her open, unseeing eyes and her gray hair, matted with blood.

My mind raced, trying to decide who to call first. I pulled out my phone and dialed 911. When the calm-voiced operator answered, all I could say was, "She's dead. Send help to the Portsmouth Apothecary," before I hung up. I stroked Trina's hair as hot tears ran down my cheeks.

A few minutes later, a gray-haired officer whose stomach strained the buttons on his shirt walked around the side of the building, gun drawn, and ordered me to move away from Trina.

I struggled to my feet and stepped out from behind the bushes. "She's dead," I whispered.

"Step over here," he commanded as he lowered his gun. When I did, he led me away from Trina. "Who are you?"

"My name is Isabella Proctor. I'm Trina's apprentice."

"Tell me what happened."

I explained I had come to talk to Trina, and that I found her, already dead.

"What time did you get here?" he asked.

I peeked at the clock on my phone. "About ten minutes ago. I called right after I found her."

He gestured to the back door of the apothecary. "Go wait over there and don't go in."

I nodded and walked with heavy legs to the door.

Another officer, a younger woman with a warm sepia complexion, walked out of the apothecary's back door with a chair. Her curly hair was pulled back in a bun, and already strands were escaping. "Sit down, miss. If you feel faint, put your head between your knees."

I did as she instructed. "I'm okay." I closed my eyes and calmed my racing mind.

Trina was gone. There would be no more afternoons laughing while working side by side making potions. No more heart-to-heart talks about what it took to be a good witch. I'd never again see her smile, full of love and acceptance of me just the way I was. I fumbled in my pocket for my phone and dialed my mother.

"Mom?" I said, my voice cracking.

"Where are you? What's wrong?"

No matter how old you were, sometimes you just needed your mother. "I'm . . . I'm at the apothecary. Trina's out back and someone's hurt her. The police are here, but . . . can you come?"

"I'll be right there."

I didn't get a chance to say thank you before she hung up.

The medical examiner arrived and inspected Trina's body. I stood up and tried to go into the quiet, dark prep room, not wanting to watch him wheel her away.

The woman officer moved in front of the door. "What are you doing?"

"Mrs. Cedar will be here in a few minutes to pick up her order."

She led me to the chair. "No one can enter the store right now. Sit down and wait here. You can't touch anything until we're done processing the scene."

I sat, wishing I had never gone to dinner last night. If I had stayed with Trina for her late-night customer, she'd still be alive today. I could have saved her.

Just as tears started streaming down my cheeks, a very pregnant woman in a brown pantsuit said, "Ms. Proctor?"

"Yes, that's me."

She pulled up another chair someone had brought out and sat with a groan. "I'm Detective Joelle Wheeler. You found Mrs. Bassett?"

I bit my lip. "Behind the bushes." I wanted to tell her more, but I couldn't make myself describe how cold her skin was, or how her blank eyes no longer held kindness.

She took a pen and notebook out of her pocket. "Was there anyone else with you?"

I shook my head. "No. It was only me. Well, and Trina . . ."

"Of course. Now, think carefully, did you see anyone in the building, or leaving when you got here?"

I hadn't seen anyone. But her question didn't even make sense. The blood had already dried, indicating Trina had been dead for a while. Was she trying to trick me, or frame me? "No, but who would have hung around all night after killing her?"

"What makes you think she'd been dead for long?" she asked.

"When I checked for her pulse, Trina was cold, and the pool of blood on the gravel had darkened and dried. The killer would have been long gone."

"The killer could have been waiting for you."

I hadn't considered that. My vision narrowed and the ground was spinning.

"Ms. Proctor?" Detective Wheeler's voice seemed far away, even though she was sitting next to me.

A hand pressed the back of my head down until I leaned over.

"Good. Stay like that for a few minutes," Detective Wheeler said, concern in her voice.

I took deep breaths until my mind cleared and the spinning subsided.

In the alley, a woman was yelling and a man was trying to calm her down. With horror, I realized the woman was my mother. I sat up and both Detective Wheeler and I looked toward the commotion.

"That's my mother. She won't let up until you let her talk to me."

"We can't let anyone else into the crime scene. You can go once I'm done with you."

She was about to ask another question when her phone rang. She answered it, but didn't say another word until the end, when she said, "I understand, sir," and hung up.

"Your mother called in a favor with the chief. He wants you released now. So, uh, those are good observations, about the crime scene I mean. Last question, and then you can go. Who would have wanted to kill her?"

"Things were a little off with Trina yesterday."

Detective Wheeler arched an eyebrow, encouraging me to continue.

"Yesterday, she had a call that sounded threatening to me. She brushed it off and wouldn't tell me anything about it. There was also a customer, Mrs. Williams, who threatened her. And yesterday afternoon, she said she couldn't come to dinner, because she had an after-hours client."

"I see." She stood up and held her hand out for me to shake. "Thank you for your cooperation. Where can I reach you?"

I looked over at my mother; she'd take me back to her house. "You can reach me at Proctor House. It's a few blocks from here."

"I'm familiar with it. Don't leave town," she commanded.

Leave town? I wasn't likely to leave my bedroom for a long time—not with a murderer on the loose.

I walked to my mother, who was scowling at another one of the many officers who had arrived on the scene. She didn't say a word as she enveloped me in a big hug.

Leaf of Faith

"Don't say anything. We'll talk once we get home," my mother whispered in my ear. "There was no need to make you watch all that."

We walked the six blocks to Proctor House in silence, her arm protectively around me.

When we entered the kitchen, an officer in a crisp uniform was sitting at the table having tea with my aunts Lily and Nadia. "Isabella, I want you to meet an old school friend of mine, Chief Dobbins," said Aunt Lily.

I shook the clammy hand of the short bald man and joined him and the aunts at the table. He flashed me a sympathetic smile that didn't touch the sadness in his eyes. "Isabella, it's good to see you again. We met when you were younger, when your Great Aunt Jemima was killed."

I imagined him with more hair and remembered him. "I'm sorry we're meeting under such bad circumstances again," I said.

"I have been a family friend for a long time, and I know you didn't kill Mrs. Bassett, but my hands are tied. Detective Wheeler has to interrogate you as thoroughly as any other suspect."

Aunt Nadia set a cup of tea and a turkey sandwich in front of me. "Eat, you'll feel better."

There was no way I could eat, although tea sounded like a good idea. I took a sip and almost choked because I wasn't expecting the whiskey she put in it. "Could I get a little milk?" I asked, hoping to mellow out the booze this early in the day. Sure, some people drank at lunch, but it didn't look like I'd ever be one of them.

I took another sip of tea; it was much better now that there was some milk in it. It hadn't occurred to me that I was a suspect, and my hands shook so much I had to put my teacup down.

"I'm also here to warn all of you it's not safe for . . ." he paused to clear his throat. "People of your persuasion right now."

He knew we were witches? He and Aunt Lily must have been extremely close at one time.

"This may be the beginning of an uptick in random violence against . . ." he faded off.

"Against who?" Aunt Lily snapped.

The chief blushed and remained silent.

"You can't even say 'witch,' can you? After all these years, you still can't bring yourself to say it." Aunt Lily scoffed.

"Now Lily, you know that I—" the chief started to say.

Aunt Lily cut him off. "I know that you're a weak man, not even able to speak the truth." She walked to the kitchen door and opened it. "Thank you for the warning."

He looked at Nadia, my mother, and me, then left without another word. Lily closed the door behind him and stormed out of the kitchen.

Never mind being close, Lily and the chief must have been in love once. It took a lot to drive my calm, sweet Aunt Lily to anger.

"What was that about?" I asked.

"Leave it for now," my mother said. "But take the warning seriously. With a murderer loose in town, it's time for you to move home."

I knew it. I was in Proctor House for less than twenty minutes, and already she was talking about me moving home.

I tried to change the subject. "How's Grandma today?"

"She's taking a nap. You'd be able to monitor her if you moved back into your old room," my mother said.

"Michelle, leave the girl alone," Aunt Nadia said.

"That's easy for you to say. You've got your daughter safe here, I'm the one who goes to bed every night terrified Isabella is going to be hurt because she lives in an apartment with one other young girl. The wards on their door won't hold back anyone determined to get in. They have hardly any protection at all!"

Every night? That seemed excessive to me. "I hardly think—"

"You don't know what it's like to worry about you every day," my mother interrupted. "There's a reason this family has always lived together. Safety. You are too young and weak to take care of yourself. Living alone is asking for trouble."

"Don't you think you're overreacting?" Aunt Nadia asked in a calm, soothing voice.

"I don't live alone; I've got Abby, and I live in a building full of friendly people. You're not being rational, Mom." I tried to keep the growing exasperation out of my voice, but it crept in. I needed to leave before we got into a real fight.

"And I say the same about your ridiculous naivete," my mom shot back.

If my mother only knew the times Abby and I had been out late at night, she'd be so much more worried. I turned the knob of the kitchen door and looked at my mother. "I don't know what Chief Dobbins is talking about. It's perfectly safe in Portsmouth."

"Tell that to Trina," my mother yelled as I walked out the back door.

Chapter 6

W hy was it the people you loved the most also frustrated you the most? I wasn't the only person this happened to, right?

I didn't usually let myself get drawn into the same old personal safety arguments, because no matter what I said, my mother wouldn't believe me. Did it seem like Portsmouth was more dangerous today? Yes, but I couldn't even remember the last time anyone was murdered here.

The walk home normally settled me down when I was frustrated with my family, but not that afternoon. The cold wind whipped my hair across my face, adding to my aggravation. By the time I got home, I decided the only way to prove she was wrong was to hit her up with facts and figures. It was also a lot easier to be mad at my mother than continue to think about Trina. Every time I closed my eyes, I saw her empty stare and I wanted to retch.

Once inside the apartment, I set the mail down on our dining table, kicked off my boots and shrugged out of my coat. Abby wouldn't be home for a few hours; now was the perfect time to reinforce the magical wards on our apartment. I placed my hands on the door, drew in my power, and focused my intention on a safe, protective home. The aunts and I put up the wards when Abby and I moved in, and now I was strengthening them. The wards were subtle. If someone tried to enter with bad intentions, they suddenly felt like they had to be somewhere else. No one would think they'd been affected by magic.

After they were as strong as I could make them, I heated myself a mug of hot cocoa and sat at the dining table with my laptop to look up murders in Portsmouth. There had been only one other murder in the last ten years, a case of domestic abuse. The man had been caught and was still in prison. It was safe to say Portsmouth was not full of murderers.

Still, one had been enough for Trina. I stared off in the distance, and all I could see was Trina's body behind the bushes. My vision blurred with unshed tears.

I closed my laptop and walked into my bedroom. I grabbed a box of tissues, the quilt my mother made me when I was a child, and Bunny Wiggles, my old stuffed bunny. It was time to relax and let my mind rest. I got comfortable on the couch and flipped on the TV. I cycled through the channels, not expecting to find anything worth watching, until I ran into an old episode of *Ben 10*. This was the show Grandma and I would watch on days I stayed home sick and the aunts were all away at work. I felt a lot like Ben when I was a kid, because we both had powers we hadn't learned how to handle. I could relate to not being able to handle things right now too.

After a few minutes my eyes grew heavy, and I didn't wake until I heard the apartment door open.

"Hey, sleepyhead," Abby said.

I rubbed my face and stretched. I hadn't planned to fall asleep, but I felt much calmer now. I must not have looked better, because once I turned to her, she immediately came to me and gave me a big hug.

"I'm so sorry. Mrs. Subramanian walked by the apothecary and then came to the café. She saw the police and asked what happened. Of course, they didn't tell her much, but she saw a body being wheeled out by the medical examiner and heard someone say Trina."

I sniffled. "It was horrible. I found her this morning." Tears streamed down my cheeks and I reached for another tissue.

Abby pulled me back into her arms. "Let it all out."

I let myself cry until I couldn't anymore. I pulled away from her, still sniffling.

"You found her? That's terrible."

I wiped my eyes and blew my nose. Guilt churned in my stomach. "She had an after-hours customer, and I left her alone so I could see Grandma."

"She never let you stay for after-hours people, did she?"

I shook my head.

"And if you tried to stay last night, she would have made you leave." Abby lifted my chin so I was looking at her instead of my lap. "This isn't your fault."

Then why did I feel like it was?

"I could have helped. I should have stayed, even if I was just outside."

"Do you know when this happened?" she asked.

"No. The police didn't tell me anything."

"She seemed like a kind person. Wacky, but nice. Who would have wanted to kill her?"

Three days ago, I would have said no one.

Leaf of Faith

Now I wasn't sure. There had been an argument in the apothecary where a jar had been broken, Mrs. Williams threatened her, and a man yelled at her on the phone so much that she was in tears. And then there were always the usual suspects to consider—family, business partners, and romantic interests.

"I have a small list."

"A list? I can't imagine making anyone mad enough at me that they might want to kill me, never mind a whole list," she said.

Talking things out with Abby lifted my mood a little. Sitting on the couch crying would not accomplish anything. Yes, I was devastated that Trina was dead, but crying was a poor substitute for figuring out who killed her. And I've never been the kind of person who waits for someone else to do things.

"If we go by every cop show we've ever watched, the husband is always the prime suspect. In this case, she's got an ex-husband, which makes him doubly suspect. Yesterday, she had an argument with Mrs. Williams, and I heard her talking on the phone to someone demanding more money. She wouldn't explain either incident. There was also broken glass in the shop that she hadn't fully swept up." I took a deep breath to steady my nerves and calm the tremor in my voice. "I don't know if that was an accident or if someone provoked a fight."

Things weren't as peaceful in her life as she let on, and I wished I had pressed her more for answers while I could.

"I can't believe your family let you come back here. Why didn't they try to keep you at their house?" she asked.

"They tried. I was there earlier, but my mother kept going on about how we're not safe, and we all need to be together."

"Again? Wasn't she harping on that last night?"

"Yes, and I walked out on her then too." I stood up and paced the length of our small living room. "I've got to go for a walk or something. Sitting here too long will drive me up a wall."

Abby yawned. "I'll come with you."

There was no way I wanted Abby to come with me. I was going to see Thea and Delia at their office, where we would talk about how our powers could find Trina's killer. We wouldn't be able to do that if Abby was there.

I shrugged into my coat. "No, don't do that. You're exhausted. I'm going to see Thea and Delia, and I'll be fine on my own."

54

Leaf of Faith

I got to Port City Tours, my cousins' tour company, in time to hold open the door for a pizza delivery guy. I followed the delicious smell of the pizza my cousins ordered for dinner and was glad I came. Thea and Delia had been running Port City Tours since we all graduated from high school. Who better to give tours of a city than that city's oldest family, right?

The business rented two small rooms six doors down from The Fancy Tart. The larger was the meeting room, where groups could book their tours at the long counter in the front, and wait for their tours to start. Comfortable chairs and a couch with a large coffee table filled the room. Posters detailing the tours available this season covered one wall. Two other walls had photos of historic Portsmouth and the local shipyard. The large window facing the street had "Port City Tours" painted on it in gold letters. Thea had taken all the photos and created the posters herself. This season they were doing the Black Heritage Trail, Strawbery Banke, and Discover Portsmouth.

I hung my coat up in the closet of the smaller room, their office, among the costumes they used when running themed tours. There were no clients, so I sat on the couch, put my feet up on the coffee table, and let out a long sigh.

Thea paid the pizza guy while Delia

pushed my feet off the table to make space for the pizza, plates, and napkins she brought.

"We heard about Trina," Delia said.

I stared out the large window, watching the cars drive by. I couldn't stand to see my cousins' concerned expressions. I was the strong cousin, the one who always kept herself together, and I didn't want them to see me falling apart.

Delia handed me a plate with two slices of mushroom pizza, my favorite. "We knew you'd show up here sooner or later."

Thea handed me a bottle of water. "You need this. You look terrible."

I gave her a wan smile. "Thanks."

I took a sip and closed my eyes. There was no way I could eat the pizza yet.

"Do you think it was magic related?" Thea asked.

"I don't know," I said.

"Thea! Maybe she doesn't want to talk about it," Delia said.

"I do. It's just . . . I don't know what to say. Talking about her seems so useless when her killer is still out there, you know what I mean?"

Delia frowned. "What else is there to do?"

"We could find out what happened to her, who killed her, and why." Figuring out what happened gave me a little spark of hope in my chest. If I knew what happened, I'd be able to make some sense out of her death, and then I would be free to grieve.

I opened my eyes and sat up. "We need to figure out what happened last night. Who's in?"

Without a second's hesitation, both my cousins said, "Me!"

Love and gratitude filled my heart. "I couldn't ask for better cousins than you two. Now, how are we going to do this without getting caught?"

Chapter 7

Thea, Delia, and I met at Port City Tours at one in the morning, and I couldn't help but laugh at Delia's outfit. She was wearing black leggings under a long black tutu and a black oversized sweater with sequins.

"What in the world are you wearing?" I asked her.

She grinned sheepishly. "We said we were going out to a party, so I had to wear party clothes. It's not my fault I didn't want to give away the plan."

I shook my head and looked from her to Thea, who was wearing more sensible black jeans and a sweater. "No party clothes for you?"

"Nothing I want to skulk around in," Thea said.

Leaf of Faith

"Your hair is going to give us away," I said to Delia. "Did you bring a hat?"

Delia said no.

"We can't go out with you like that. It will be obvious who you are to anyone that's still out tonight. Do you have a hat in with your costumes?" I asked.

Delia shook her head slowly, but then her eyes widened and she walked into the costume closet. She pulled out a large black shawl and wrapped it around her head, hijab style. "Are we ready?"

My heart thudded in my chest. I worried about getting caught, but also worried about what we might find. Most murder victims were killed by people they knew. What if someone I knew was a murderer? I decided it was better to know than to wonder for the rest of my life. "Let's go."

We walked quickly, not speaking because we didn't want to call any attention to ourselves on the quiet, dark streets. We decided to walk through the back alleys as much as possible, and when we startled a cat, Delia let out a short scream. Without thinking, Thea and I both shushed her, adding to the noise.

After we took a moment to calm down, we moved on.

We made it to the apothecary with only one incident of banging into trash cans, and thankfully, we didn't arouse anyone's suspicions. I held up the crime scene tape for Thea and Delia. Thea led us along the edge of the small courtyard behind the stores, trying not to disturb anything.

Delia had promised to practice her darkness spell this afternoon to make sure it was strong enough to at least block the light from our flashlights. "Go ahead and cast now," I whispered to Delia.

In the dark, I could barely make out her arms moving in a wide circle. "This is the best I can do," Delia said. "We should be safe if we stick to using flashlights."

I unlocked the back door to the apothecary. "Okay. I'm going to check the office, you two focus on the shop itself. Let me know if you find anything."

In the office, Trina's desk had been emptied, and papers and books were strewn everywhere. Trina would never have left for the night without tidying up. I scanned the papers on the desk. They were the custom order forms for the last four or five years. Who would be interested in the special orders Trina had created for past customers? It would be a lot easier to ask what services we had available.

The papers on the floor had been pulled out of the open filing cabinet. They were recipes for various potions that Trina and I could make.

Clearly someone was searching for a specific potion. I gently picked one up by the corner to inspect the oily footprint on it. The recipe was for creativity oil, but apparently the killer didn't care about creativity.

We refused to make many types of potions. The list was about what you might expect. We never made anything that allowed one person to control another, we didn't make anything that did the "grant me three wishes" sort of jinn thing, and we didn't make anything that would allow people to get rich quick. We had our ethical standards, as Trina always reminded me, and we never used our work to help one person gain advantage over others. These potions were far too dangerous in the wrong hands.

If you were having problems with your gout flaring up, or needed a good tonic to help you sleep, then we were definitely the women for you. This wellness vibe helped spur Trina's "do no harm and don't treat without permission mindset." She saw herself as an adjunct to the medical field, or sometimes a replacement for it.

All the drawers in her desk had been pulled out and dumped as well. Books had been knocked off her bookshelf. I itched to clean up and put everything away, but we couldn't let the police know we'd been here. I flashed my light around the room one more time and then went out to the shop.

"Find anything?" I whispered to Delia. From the outside, Delia's spell made the apothecary look dark and empty, but on the off chance someone was walking by, I didn't want them to hear me.

"The cash register is open, and it's mostly empty," Delia said.

I flashed my light to the register. There were no bills, but the coins were still separated in their slots. "If Trina was going to make a bank run, she'd take the bills and coins. It looked like she left all the money in the till." It wouldn't have been too much, maybe a few hundred dollars. Not enough to make it worth breaking in here or killing her.

"There are a bunch of smashed jars as well. It looks like someone was furious and wanted to take it out on her business," Delia whispered.

My heart sank as I took in the complete destruction of the shop. It would be months before I could remake all the potions that had been destroyed, and it would cost more than the shop probably had. I didn't know when I'd be able to replace the rest of the merchandise.

Then again, it was possible it wasn't even going to be my problem. Trina had never talked about what she would do for retirement, or who she might leave the business to. It was certainly too early in my training for her to think about me taking over.

"Thea is checking out the prep room," said Delia.

We joined Thea and coughed at the smell of isopropyl alcohol.

"Did they break every bottle in here too?" Delia asked.

I ran my flashlight along the storage shelves and saw the same destruction as in the main shop. Broken glass everywhere, potions and herbs thrown around, and so many supplies wasted.

"I agree with Delia. Someone was furious and decided to ruin everything for Trina," said Thea.

"I think they did that the moment they cracked her skull. This was overkill," I said.

Thea gave my hand a squeeze. "Do you want to go investigate what happened outside?"

No, I didn't want to, but I knew we had to. "We can't get close to the bloodstain or where she was dragged, but we should go into the greenhouse."

"That's okay with me," said Delia. "I don't want to get too close to the place she died. It gives me shivers even being all the way over here."

We walked outside and I locked the door. Delia snapped her fingers, and the spell over the apothecary vanished.

"Can you cast that spell again for the greenhouse?" I asked.

"I can, but it's all glass, so we should be fast. The spell was already fading in the shop, and we were only there for maybe ten minutes. I'll have to ramp up the intensity for the greenhouse. I'll only be able to hold the spell for a couple minutes. After that, we run the risk of being seen," Delia said.

Right. We'd have to be quick. Once I felt the spell click into place, I opened the greenhouse door. The smell of alcohol hit me like a brick and I sputtered.

"What the heck?" asked Delia.

"More alcohol. But why?" I asked.

We walked in, and once we trained our flashlights on the wilting plants, it was obvious.

"Who would do this?" I cried. Every single plant had been hit with alcohol and was now dying. I ran my flashlight up and down the two walkways that ran the length of the greenhouse and saw nothing but dying plants.

"Let's go before we breathe too much of this," Thea said.

Delia snapped her fingers to release the second darkness spell. We left quickly, walked around the edge of the courtyard again, snuck under the crime scene tape and walked in silence.

After a few minutes, the smell of alcohol

left my nose, and the wooziness cleared out of my head. "What happened last night?" I asked, but no one answered me. My cousins were as clueless as I was.

We returned to their office and went inside. It was the best place for us to talk privately. "I don't know what happened there, but someone was really angry. I could feel it in the air, even a day after," Delia said.

"Could you feel anything specific? Like who it was or what they were after?" I asked.

Delia shook her head. "It's fading fast, too. By morning I won't be able to feel anything."

"Did we learn anything?" Thea asked.

"The murderer was searching for something—the office was a mess, and files were all over the place. I'd have to tidy it up before I could figure out what was missing," I said.

"Once the police are done, I'm sure they'll let you in to tidy up. You'll have to, won't you? Too many people rely on you and Trina"—Thea stopped speaking for a moment—"on you now, I guess, for what they need."

My shoulders sagged under the thought that people would be counting on me. Sure, Trina let me do a lot of the simple work, but being responsible for everything seemed too much.

I jumped up from the couch. "I've got to go. I'll see you tomorrow for lunch?"

Before they could even answer, I ran out the door as though I could run from my responsibilities to Trina's clients.

One block away from the shop, blue lights broke the darkness of the night as a car pulled up next to me. I kept walking while the car matched my pace.

"Excuse me," the driver said through the open passenger side window.

I turned to see a man holding out a badge. "I'm Detective Steve Palmer. Can I speak to you for a moment?" he asked.

I stopped walking. "It's cold, make it quick."

He smiled. "The car is warm. I'll drive you home."

A warm car sounded great right about now, but a ride from the police after I'd just broken into a crime scene didn't sound like the smartest thing to do. On the other hand, would I seem guilty if I didn't take him up on his offer? Should I call a lawyer? Could I afford a lawyer? Probably not. There was no good answer here, so I opted to at least be out of the icy wind.

"Good evening, Detective Palmer. Do you often prowl the streets of Portsmouth looking for women to drive home?"

Now that I was in the car, I could make out more of his features. When he smiled, his brown eyes crinkled. He looked in his mid-twenties, with short brown hair and a serious case of five o'clock shadow. He laughed. "No. But there was a murder in the area last night, and I was hoping the perp would revisit the scene of the crime."

My eyes widened. I hadn't even considered that when we came up with our plan to search the apothecary for clues. I hoped my distress would seem like sadness over Trina's death and not over nearly being caught.

"Yes, I know. I was Trina's apprentice."

"Interesting," he murmured as he pulled a notebook out of his jacket pocket and flipped it open. "You're Isabella Proctor?"

"Yes."

"What a coincidence. I was going to speak to you later today, but now I can ask you questions while I drive you home."

He put the car into drive and headed for my apartment. I hadn't told him my address, but he already knew where to go.

"I'm taking over the case from Detective Wheeler, because she's gone into early labor. Do you have any ideas about who might have wanted Mrs. Bassett dead? You worked most closely with her, and I thought you'd have some valuable insight."

I turned toward him. "I do. In fact, I've got a list. Trina was having problems with several people over the past week. I'd never noticed her having trouble like this before. Her ex-husband, Frank, is at the top of my list, but Caroline Arneson and Mrs. Williams threatened her today. We've got a troubling client that Trina swore wasn't a danger, but I'm not sure. Her name is Agatha. Trina had a late-night client last night that I don't know, and I heard someone demanding money from her over the phone."

He turned the car into my parking lot. "That's a considerable list. I'll look into them. In the meanwhile, Miss Proctor, stay safe. It's clear you've given this a lot of thought and it's best for civilians to leave investigating to the police. Murder investigations aren't for amateurs—they can get hurt."

I got out of his car. *Amateur*. Ha! He had no idea how well I could protect myself if I needed to.

Chapter 8

I went straight up to my apartment. The lights were out when I unlocked the door, and the entire building was silent.

I turned on the living room light and looked around, happy to be home.

Abby had tidied up before she went to bed—dishes were in the drying rack and the carpets had vacuum tracks.

I was too wound up to go to sleep, so I drew myself a bath and poured in a bit of calendula oil. The delicate scent was exactly what I needed to release the pent-up stress I was carrying. I slipped down in the water until my chin rested on the surface and willed all my muscles to relax. The tension in my shoulders released, and I allowed the hot water to work its own kind of magic on my muscles.

If the murderer was searching for something, it was because Trina wouldn't give it to him. Or her. Or them. Trina had strict rules about the potions we provided, and she wouldn't deviate from them. It looked to me like she turned the killer down in the shop, where they tried to intimidate her by breaking things. When that didn't work, they chased her outside, killed her, then decided to search the office.

I had to stop thinking like this, or I was never going to get to sleep. I flicked my hand at the candle on the counter to light it, and turned off the bathroom lights the same way. I stared at the candle, meditating in the tub.

As usual, I fell asleep during my meditation and woke feeling cold and pruney. I turned the light on and drained the water. A quick hot shower to warm up again, and I'd be ready for a good night's sleep.

Two minutes into my shower, Abby knocked on the bathroom door. "Isabella, I've got to get ready for work. Are you almost done?"

Oh, broomsticks! I had no idea I'd slept for that long. "Yeah—give me two seconds to dry off." I hopped out of the shower, did the minimum drying off, wrapped a towel around myself, scooped up my black skulking-around clothes, and opened the door.

"You fell asleep in the bathtub again,

didn't you?" she asked.

"Yeah, I did. I'm going to bed now though."

The sunshine filtering through the yellow curtains filled my bedroom with a warm light that woke me up. I stretched and enjoyed the warm, cozy feeling of being wrapped up in my blankets. I was well-rested and had a million questions about what happened to Trina. I had decided as I was drifting off last night that I should talk to Chief Dobbins today, see if I could get any information out of him. I wasn't going to straight up ask him to tell me everything he knew, but I was good at getting people to talk.

After I left my apartment, I ran into Mrs. Thompson on the stairs. Today she was wearing her red wool peacoat with matching gloves and boots.

"Hello, Isabella," she said.

"Hi, Mrs. Thompson. Let me help you with that bag."

I took the full bag of groceries from her — at seventy-eight, she didn't need to lug them upstairs herself. She usually shopped every other day, saying the walk did her good. She must have picked this apartment for its closeness to the grocery store.

"Thank you, dear. I decided to get more than usual because there's a storm forecasted, and I don't think I'll be getting out of the apartment for the rest of the week."

"Sounds ominous. You let me know if you run out of anything, and I'll pick it up," I said. She was like the grandma I never had—sweet, loving, and kind. My grandma, on the other hand, was often the emotional equivalent to stepping on a Lego.

I brought her groceries into her apartment and set them on the dining table. Her apartment had the same layout as mine, but the antique furniture, drapes, and art made hers look like a home compared to the cheap, first-apartment aesthetic Abby and I had. "Can I do anything for you while I'm here?" I asked. Sometimes she had a jar that wouldn't open, or needed me to take a piece of china down from the top shelf. Life must be tough at just over five feet tall.

"No, dear. Thank you, though."

Jameson, her black short-haired cat, rubbed against my leg, and I bent down to pet him. He purred for me when I scratched between his ears. "Who's a good boy?" I asked, which got me more purring. I straightened. "I'll see you both soon."

On my way out, I heard music from the apartment on the other side of mine. Today the Stanleys were listening to Sinatra. Mrs. Stanley said Sinatra was the music they dated to, and they always felt young when listening to him.

Outside, I understood what Mrs. Thompson was talking about. I could smell that snow would fall in a few hours. First things first; I went to see Chief Dobbins.

The Portsmouth police station was a curious mix of modern and classic. The building itself was one of the old brick behemoths from the eighteenth century, complete with massive columns flanking the large front door, and a waiting room that reflected the Georgian exterior. Past the reception area, though, it was sleek and modern.

The receptionist called the chief to announce me, and he came right out to greet me. The chief was about as old as the aunts, which made sense, since I was fairly sure he and Aunt Lily dated a long time ago. He had the look of too many donuts and not enough chasing people down the street that lots of middle-aged men get, and the straining buttons on his shirt said he hadn't come to terms with it yet. He smiled warmly at me. I thought that was a bit strange, but who was I to judge. He walked me to his office personally, and I felt special, like he was showing me off. Once I entered the office, he closed the door. Commendations, award plaques, and photos of the chief with prominent people covered the walls of his office. A laptop and two large monitors rested on the oak desk he took a seat behind.

Once I sat and accepted his offer of coffee—how had I managed to leave my apartment without eating breakfast or having any coffee—I got down to business. "Well, Chief, I was wondering how long it would take you to finish the investigation at the apothecary. I'd like to keep the shop open at least long enough to allow our clients to have what they need until they can find another herbalist."

Chief Dobbins nodded. "Commendable. But I'm not sure that's going to be feasible. You didn't get a good look at the shop, but there isn't much left inside that hasn't been destroyed. And the plants in the greenhouse are probably all dead by now."

I knew that, so it was time to pull out my high school acting class talent and fake surprise.

"Really? There must be some things that can be salvaged. I mean, it would take a long time to destroy everything. And the plants can withstand a few days of neglect before they droop."

He shook his head. "Almost everything was smashed, and the plants had alcohol poured over them. They were dying yesterday."

I covered my mouth with my hand, feigning shock. "Who would do that? I mean, wasn't it bad enough they . . . they killed Trina, without destroying her business too?"

He leaned forward, conspiratorially. "You didn't hear this from me, but I think that was the plan all along. A person doesn't take that long to destroy something in the middle of the night, after having killed someone, unless they're holding a serious grudge."

I thought about that for a minute. I couldn't imagine what Trina had done to provoke so much rage.

"Are you sure that was the order of events? I mean, how can you tell when the shop was destroyed?"

The chief leaned back in his chair and laced his fingers behind his head, getting ready to give me a lecture. "Are you interested in police work? We could always use more young women on the force. It gives us a better reputation with the town—you know, it looks like we're taking a softer approach."

I was not interested in police work, because it focused on the letter of the law rather than justice. But he didn't need to know that right now. "I feel like I have a lot of options open to me, and while police work wasn't something I considered, having a closer view of what you do is much more interesting than I had ever expected." And my mother said I wasn't diplomatic.

He put his elbows on the desk. "There are a few clues that point to her being killed first."

I widened my eyes but didn't say anything. The best way to get someone to share information with you is to be quiet and let them fill the silence.

"Clue number one: she didn't have any glass or oil on her shoes. Clue number two: we have a fairly accurate time of death based on her body temperature, and that was about forty-five minutes before the time on the broken clock in her office. About one thirty that morning. Clue number three: if she had walked in to see someone destroying her business, she would have tried to fight them off, and other than her head wound, she didn't have any other injuries."

That certainly seemed like a lot of evidence. Why hadn't I noticed any of that? I was thinking about what I had missed when the chief said, "I'm sorry. This must be too much for you to think about so soon. Let me bring you out to the lobby and get you out of here."

It was her body, I realized. If I had examined her shoes or her hands, I might have noticed the lack of evidence. I felt useless; all I did was sit with her, waiting for the police to arrive when I could have been looking for clues. Next time. Oh, goddess, I hope there's no next time. If I never have to do this again, that would be great.

Chapter 9

It's a good thing the chief sent me out when he did, because I had to work at three. If I rushed, I would clock in just in time.

In The Fancy Tart's kitchen, Bethany drew her eyebrows together. "Didn't you get Abby's message? You didn't have to come in today."

That was kind, but I needed the money. Plus, if I kept my mind busy, I wouldn't spend my time crying or remembering Trina behind the bushes.

"I didn't. I'd rather be here, keeping busy, and helping out."

Bethany nodded, seeming to understand how I felt. "Well then, you can help me clean up the kitchen. We're done baking, and once it's clean, I'm going home. Start with the work surfaces."

Cleaning and sanitizing the kitchen benches was the most mindless job in the bakery. I grabbed paper towels and a spray bottle of sanitizer from the shelf of cleaning supplies. The sanitizer hissed out of the nozzle and floated down to the table. I tore a paper towel off the roll and rhythmically wiped down the stainless steel work surface.

"I met Trina when she opened the apothecary. She knew how to make her products, and she assumed the rest of the business would take care of itself." Bethany chuckled. "She was so wrong!"

"What happened?" I asked.

"I couldn't stand by and watch the young woman throw her dream away for want of a little advice, so I helped. In the first year the apothecary was open, I spent more time working in her business than in my own."

"And who ran the bakery?" I asked.

Bethany sighed. "My husband was alive then, and my son was still talking to us. They ran the bakery while I worked with Trina."

I had no idea Bethany knew Trina well. "Trina never mentioned your help in getting up and running. She always seemed so good at managing everything about the business."

"She picked up the business side quickly,

and she's never been one to admit needing help."

Maybe that was what got her killed. If she had asked for help, or told me what the problem was, we could have worked together to fix it. After all, she was family, and I'm sure Grandma or the aunts would have pitched in too.

"Do you know how to run her business?" I asked.

"I can balance the books and keep track of inventory. Why?"

I stopped washing the table and looked up. "We have customers who rely on us, and I'm afraid I won't be able to help them on my own. I was wondering . . ."

Bethany shook her head. "You're getting too far ahead of yourself. Did she tell you that you would inherit the business? Or have you seen her will?"

"No. We never talked about it."

"There's a strong chance she might leave it to her ex-husband. His business would merge well with hers."

I hadn't considered that. Frank and Trina had been divorced long enough that they had circled around and become friends again. His tiny mail-order crystal business would have been a good addition to the apothecary. "That's a good point. I still feel responsible for the customers though."

Leaf of Faith

Omar, one of the new hires, stuck his curly head through the doorway. "We need some help up front."

"I'll go," I said. It would be faster for Bethany to finish cleaning the kitchen than to wait on customers.

The first person I waited on was Mrs. Newcomb, Trina's favorite customer. She was in her midsixties and had a raspy voice from smoking. Trina made her a honey-based throat soother that Mrs. Newcomb claimed worked better than anything her doctors gave her.

"There you are, doll," Mrs. Newcomb rasped. "I was hoping to see you today, because I wanted to tell you how sorry I am for your loss. For our loss. I've come to rely on our Tuesday afternoons together, just gabbing." She looked off in the distance before she continued, "And you, what are you going to do? You're keeping the business open, right?"

As we talked, Omar helped several other customers. I often thought Mrs. Newcomb would talk forever, if she didn't have to pause to cough. I put her standard order in a bag. "Thank you. That means a lot to me. Coffee cake muffin?"

She took the bag from my hand. "You take care, doll. If you need anything, you call me right away. Trina would want me to take care of you."

She walked to the cash register and I

turned away from the line for a moment, blinking back tears. I guess you never realized how much people cared about you until there was trouble.

I faced the customers and saw Mrs. Thompson next in line.

"How nice to see you again," I said. "What can I get for you this afternoon?"

"I'll have a nice rhubarb square and a cup of the rooibos tea. After all that's been going on lately, I need to relax and sit quietly for a while."

"Why don't you go take a seat, and I'll bring your order," I offered.

She chose a small table in the corner, away from the door. "Best seat in the house for chilly days," I said as I set her tea and snack in front of her. "No drafts, and it's easy to sit quietly if you want." I set a small, wrapped package on the table. "Some treats for Jameson straight from the kitchen."

She patted my hand. "You're too good to us. One day I'll have to do something kind for you. Don't let me keep you from your work."

I got to the counter in time to help Agatha, the last person in line, with her order. Apparently, she wanted an éclair, but her invisible friend Alice said she should eat a salad once in a while. Agatha insisted she would, if they weren't in a bakery and said it would be rude to ask for something we didn't serve. I'd heard these conversations often

Leaf of Faith

enough that I knew the éclair would win out. I set one on a plate for her. She always chose a different drink, though. I waited for her, or them, to make up their minds.

I worried about Agatha. Sometimes she didn't seem to know what she was doing.

In the end, salted caramel hot cocoa won out over Korean salad water. I made her cocoa and brought it to the register. "You go sit and I'll bring your order to you." I had some questions for her about where she was the night Trina was killed.

Once she chose a table, I set her cocoa in front of her.

"When will the apothecary open up?" she asked.

"I'm not sure. The police are still examining it for clues. I think it should be open in the next couple days, though. Do you need anything?"

She nodded. "Yup. Yup. I do. I need some ashwagandha because"—her voice rose in anger—"Alice is getting to be too loud in my head. Salad water with an éclair? That's wrong."

I sat down across the table from her, hoping I could calm her down and ask her a few questions. "I can help you as soon as the store opens. I promise I'll call, and you can come down to pick up what you need. Can I ask you a question?"

She blinked in confusion. "Agatha or Alice?"

"Well, I suppose the both of you. Can you tell me where you were the night Trina was killed?"

"I was at home, sleeping under my bed. I don't know where Alice was."

"Why were you sleeping under your bed? It can't possibly be as comfortable as sleeping on your mattress, can it?"

She laughed. "Alice says the bed is more comfortable too. That's why she insists on sleeping on it. As long as I let her have the bed, she leaves me alone until morning." Her eyes widened and she whispered, "That means she doesn't have an alibi. Do you think she did it?"

My heart ached for Agatha. Whatever was wrong with her, Trina hadn't been able to fix with a potion. It was time for her to seek more traditional medicine. "I don't know. Can you ask her?"

Agatha closed her eyes for a moment, opened them, and said, "Alice says she was home all night. I don't know if I believe her though. She's sneaky and has gotten into trouble before."

"How does she get into trouble without you?"

Agatha looked at me like I was an idiot. "She can't. We share the body so I am with her wherever she goes. I don't remember going somewhere with her, not until I realize I'm in different clothes or unless there's something wrong."

"What do you mean, wrong?"

"Like, if someone said they saw me somewhere I didn't remember being."

"Do you have any roommates? Maybe they'd know if you went out that night."

Agatha looked at her cocoa. "No roommates. Alice drives them away."

There was no way I was going to get much more out of Agatha. Maybe Palmer could, or maybe she'd be more coherent once I replenished her potions.

"As soon as I can, I'll get you what you need. In the meantime, go see my grandma. She's got a big medicinal garden and can help you."

She looked at me, distrust in her eyes. "I don't take medicine from just anyone."

"If you know Trina, you probably know my grandma, Esther Proctor."

Agatha's face lit up. "You're Esther's granddaughter? No wonder you're all red around the edges."

"You can see my aura?"

She scoffed. "Not me, silly. Alice can see auras, not me. She says your aura is red." She leaned in toward me and whispered, "That's not good. You take too many risks, and you're in danger."

My mouth went dry, because she might be right. "I, uh, I have to go now. I have other work to do." I walked unsteadily to the kitchen and sat on a stool.

"What's wrong?" Bethany asked as she put her arm through the sleeve of her coat. She was going home, and I didn't want to bother her with my theory about Agatha having killed Trina. "It's nothing."

Bethany took her coat off and came to stand beside me. She took my hand in hers. "You shouldn't lie."

Before I could answer her, my phone rang. My mother was on the phone, and she was talking fast and soft. "I can't understand you. Slow down and talk louder."

"Grandma took more of your potion, and she's making a scene. We're at The Crispy Biscuit. Meet us at home—we need help calming her down."

The potion I made for Grandma wasn't made with anything known for strong interactions. In fact, the ingredients were all used in food. On the other hand, though my mother often overreacted, she was not one to panic outright. If she said they needed help, then things were bad. "I'm at work. I'll be there as soon as I

Leaf of Faith

can. Do you need me to help you get her home?"

"No. Just get home fast."

Bethany furrowed her brow. "Problems?"

I put my phone in my pocket. "My grandmother isn't doing well, and I need to go see her. I'm sorry, I promise I'll make up the hours.

She took her coat off. "Go, don't worry about us."

I got home before the rest of the family and started going through Grandma's room. She would be mad if she knew I was doing this, but I had to find what caused the interaction. I searched through her drawers, her closet, her bathroom, and even under her bed, and found nothing suspicious.

Where would Grandma hide something? Before I could find anything, I heard Grandma yelling as my mother and aunts walked her up the driveway.

I rushed down to the kitchen to see the aunts forcing Grandma into the house.

"We can't leave him behind. Don't close the door until we let him in," Grandma wailed.

"I have no idea what she's talking about.

There is no man with us, and no one followed us home," my mother said.

"Hallucinating?" I asked.

"Yes," Aunt Lily said.

Aunt Nadia and my mother finally succeeded in wrestling Grandma down into a chair because they agreed to leave the kitchen door open. Grandma stared at the door silently, as if waiting for someone to walk in.

"What's going on?" I asked.

"When she insisted we save a spot for him at the table, we were a little worried. The longer it took him to show up, the more agitated she got. She wouldn't let us order until he got there. We compromised by ordering some appetizers first, but when she yelled about needing to keep the restaurant door open, we knew we had to leave," Aunt Nadia said.

Grandma looked away from the door at me. "Is that you, Isabella?"

I pulled the chair in front of Grandma and sat. I took her cold, clammy hands in mine. "Yes, Grandma, it's me. Can you tell me who we're waiting for?"

Grandma pulled her hands out of mine abruptly. "He didn't tell me his name, because it's a secret. I know he has important things to tell us—things that will save lives."

The wind slammed our open kitchen door

and we all jumped.

"He's here," Grandma whispered.

She closed her eyes and began to shake. I grabbed her hand again, and she squeezed it tight. After a minute, she stopped shaking and opened her eyes. "He's gone. We can close the door."

Aunt Lily shut the door and then locked it, something we hardly ever did when we were at home. The wards on our house were centuries old and kept us safe.

"Mom, are you okay?" my mother asked.

Grandma sat up. "I think so. He said I was in danger."

"What kind of danger?" Aunt Nadia asked.

"I don't know. He left too quickly," Grandma said. She sagged in her chair, barely able to keep her eyes open. "Help me up to bed. I need to rest."

Aunt Lily helped her up, and she and I each supported one side of Grandma as we slowly walked her to her bedroom. She lay down on her bed with a sigh of relief. "Maybe I'll feel better tomorrow."

I wanted one more answer from her. "Grandma, who were you talking to?" She didn't answer, because she was fast asleep already.

Aunt Lily pulled me out of the bedroom. "What else was in that potion you gave her?"

"Nothing. It was lemon, rosemary, and juniper heated in water."

"Are you sure?"

"What are you saying? Do you think I did this?"

Aunt Lily ran her fingers through her hair. "No. I guess not. It's just that she was fine yesterday, then she took your potion."

I frowned. "But she wasn't fine. She was exhausted and very much not herself. The problem is with whatever made her that way, interacting with my potion. You need to scour the house and find anything new she might be taking, before it's too late."

Chapter 10

Once I made sure the aunts were okay without me, I headed out. My plan was to go back to the café until I realized my family had probably left the restaurant without paying. I mean, who would stop them when they were trying to get a raving woman out of the place?

They had gone to The Crispy Biscuit, a local hot spot that served breakfast all day. I pushed the glass door open and was engulfed by the smell of bacon and coffee. Were they competition to The Fancy Tart? Sort of, although we don't serve full sit-down meals like the Biscuit does.

The Biscuit also had a very different atmosphere. The red-and-white upholstered booths were cozy and complemented the eclectic and ever-changing art collection on display. A beautiful seascape oil painting could be hung next to a velvet Elvis. You never knew what you were going to see next.

At the servers' station, I was happy to see my friend Emma.

"Hey, Isabella, how's your grandmother?" Emma asked.

It was good to have an understanding friend. "She's resting now. She's on a new medication, and she's having a reaction to it." *Close enough.*

Emma frowned. "That happens. I hope she gets it worked out quickly. She looked really upset."

I gave her arm a quick squeeze. "Thanks. I'm sure she will. The aunts will take care of her. I'm actually here to pay their bill. I don't imagine anyone remembered to leave some money on the table when Grandma started yelling, did they?"

"No, they didn't. They didn't order much, so I paid for it out of my tips."

Her kindness made me smile. Sure, we've been friends since the sixth grade, but tips aren't great this early in the year. "Wow, that's kind of you. How much was it?"

She held up her hand like she didn't want to take my money, and I slid a twenty-dollar bill between two of her fingers.

"No, that's not necessary. And it wasn't that much," she said. She tried to return the bill. I put my hands in my pockets.

"Keep talking and I'll add more to it," I warned.

She smiled. "Fine. I'll get you back for this."

The large tip was fair, because any time there's a disturbance, other people leave quickly and tips suffer. At least this way, I was helping to make up for the problem Grandma caused.

"So, does your grandma do this a lot? I don't remember her being the screaming type," Emma asked.

I shook my head. "No. She's been tired lately, and at least until today, she's been as lucid as you or me. It'll be a bit before she goes out again though. What did she say?"

"It was the weirdest thing. It's like she had Alzheimer's and thought someone she used to know was going to join them. She insisted on having another place setting, and when this imaginary person didn't show up, she got agitated and insisted we keep the door open." She sighed. "I love your grandma, but it's too cold outside to keep the door open. When we didn't, she flipped out."

Emma's voice cracked with sadness. Of course she didn't want to upset Grandma, but she had responsibilities too. "Understandable."

"Your mother and aunts practically had to drag her out of here. She kept saying that he wouldn't be able to find her if they left."

I frowned. Hallucinations were never good. "Well, thanks again. I appreciate you taking care of my family like this."

How could I figure out what was wrong with Grandma? I wished I could ask Trina what to do. I shoved my icy hands into my coat pockets and walked to The Fancy Tart. There was nothing for me to do to help Grandma, so I could at least take care of my responsibilities to work and Bethany.

Thoughts about Grandma's taking a bad turn and Trina's death were swirling in my head, and I didn't hear Mrs. Williams calling to me until she had caught up with me on the sidewalk.

"Oh, I'm sorry. I guess I was preoccupied." I stopped walking because she was winded.

She put a hand on my arm. "I wanted to tell you how very sorry I am about, well, you know."

Was she sorry? Now was the perfect time to ask her about what she and Trina were arguing about. "Thank you. It's such a senseless tragedy. It makes me feel like none of us are safe here anymore. In fact, I noticed she had been arguing with people lately—a lot of people."

Mrs. Williams tried for a surprised expression, but I knew better. I'd heard her threatening Trina. "What do you mean?" she asked.

I took her hand in mine. "People like you, coming into the shop and telling Trina she had until the night she was killed to make something right."

She tried to shake her hand loose. I didn't let go. "I didn't realize you'd heard that."

"Did you have a reason to kill her?"

To my surprise, she laughed. "Over a double charge on my credit card? It doesn't seem worth it, does it?"

"It all depends on how much it was, I suppose."

"Ten dollars. If she didn't reverse the charge, I was going to call my credit card company. They would have taken it from there, but I don't think they send out hit men for a ten-dollar issue." She wrenched her hand out of mine. "Honestly, what you young people will say. You don't have a shred of decency. You can bet I won't return to the apothecary, not if you're going to accuse me of murder. And expect a call from my credit card company."

She walked away, muttering about kids these days.

I should have been worried about losing a

customer. I wasn't. I'd never have to pick out each individual flower for her again.

Before I got to The Fancy Tart, Trina's lawyer called to announce the reading of her will. I had to be there because I was, as he put it, a major beneficiary. Trina and I never talked about her will, and I was surprised I was in it. She was only fifty-four when she died; I guess she never thought she needed to tell me.

The bakery was empty, except for Omar. We closed at five o'clock in the evening, and the hour before that was usually dead.

"Hey, Omar. I'm back."

Omar looked at me and shook his head. "Oh, no. Bethany gave me strict instructions if you came back." He reached into the display case and withdrew two éclairs and put them in a bag. "I was to give you these and send you home."

I smiled and took the bag. I've never been one to turn down éclairs. Someday I'd have the hips to prove it, but not today. Today I could eat them without penalty.

"She said you should go home and relax."

I folded the top of the bag over. "She's not wrong there. I'll fill you in the next time I see you."

"Oh, one more thing. You had a phone message from your grandmother."

From Grandma? She had been sound asleep an hour ago. Omar handed me a piece of paper that read, "I had a nap and am feeling much better now."

I was relieved she felt better and was sure the aunts would keep a close eye on her tonight. I jammed the note in my pocket, thanked Omar and headed for home, a good movie, and two éclairs for dinner.

The next morning, I left my apartment early, wanting to get to the grocery store before the storm Mrs. Thompson warned me about arrived.

Detective Palmer was in my driveway, leaning against his unmarked Dodge Charger. I hadn't noticed how good he looked in his leather coat and jeans when he had driven me home. The sweater he wore was tight enough to show he was a man who took going to the gym seriously. I shook the idea out of my head. Until he didn't see me as a suspect, I couldn't treat him as anything but a cop.

"Good morning, Detective. How may I help you?" I asked.

He straightened up and opened his passenger door. "Miss Proctor, I'd like you to come with me to the station. We have some questions."

That sounded ominous, and I hesitated. The sooner he excluded me, though, the sooner he'd be on the trail of Trina's real killer. I bit my lip. "Okay. I'm going to need some coffee before we get there."

"We have coffee at the station," he said.

I scowled at him. "You forget where I work. Burned, day-old brown water will *not* be sufficient. I'm going to need real coffee." I smiled, hoping he'd pick up on my banter. "I need strength to get through answering more of your questions."

He seemed to take that as a compliment, because he smiled at me. "Okay. We'll get two from a drive-through." He gestured for me to sit in the front seat.

I suppose it was good that he didn't have me sitting in the back seat, like a real suspect. Then again, maybe he thought I didn't pose any danger to him, and the risk of having me up front was zero. Either way, I was glad to not look guilty as we drove.

"Thank you. Maybe we could get breakfast too?"

One of his eyebrows lifted. "From The Fancy Tart?"

"Where else? Do you think I'm a pastry traitor?"

"Of course not. I wouldn't take pastry from just any bakery. I'll take your offer and raise your coffee size to a large, my treat."

This was going well. A little flirtatious banter never hurt before having to defend my actions. I was a little surprised he went along with it though. We stopped at The Fancy Tart for coffee and Danishes, and were at the station in under fifteen minutes.

He led me to a bleak interrogation room. One table, two chairs, a digital recorder, and a one-way mirror were all that was in the industrial gray room. The fluorescent light above the table buzzed.

He motioned to the chair that faced the mirror. "Have a seat."

We both sat, and I willed my racing heart to slow down.

"I am going to tape this interview for future reference," he said after he turned the recorder on.

"Fine. Ask me anything you like."

He took a bite of his Danish I let him choose from the bag and then leaned back, relaxing. We've all seen enough cop shows to know that the interrogation room was the equivalent of a stage, and that it was all an act. He was relaxing to encourage me to relax. It was working, too.

"First, we should just talk, get the basics about your life down. Can you state your full name and occupation for the tape?"

"Starting off with the easy questions? My name is Isabella Prudence Proctor. Please don't tease me about Prudence. It's not my fault. If you wanted to threaten to arrest my mother for such a horrible middle name, there might be another pastry in it for you," I said.

He chuckled. "And your occupation?"

"I work the counter at The Fancy Tart Café here in Portsmouth."

"Any other jobs?" he asked.

"I am an apprentice, sorry, I was an apprentice for Trina Bassett at the Portsmouth Apothecary."

"Nothing else?" he prompted.

"No. Nothing else." When would I have had time to have a third job? Maybe if I got paid for a sleep study.

"I've seen you working at the bakery, probably too many times than is good for my health. Tell me about the internship," he said.

I sighed. I didn't want to talk about Trina; her death was still too fresh in my heart. "There are many paths to becoming an herbalist, and I chose the apprenticeship route. It helped that Trina was a distant relative, and she was willing to teach me."

"And what did she pay you?"

"Like a lot of internships, she didn't pay me anything. Then again, I didn't pay her for teaching me. It was a mutually beneficial arrangement that didn't involve the transfer of money."

He looked at me skeptically. "There's a lot of room for her to take advantage of you in that situation."

"I suppose there was, but that was not my experience. She was patient with me, wasn't upset when I left home and had to find another job to pay the bills."

"When you began as her intern, you were still living with your family?"

I nodded.

"Please answer for the tape," he reminded me.

"Oh, sorry. Yes. When I started the internship, I lived at home and didn't need another job."

"Why move? Wasn't it easier to live at home?" he asked.

I took a sip of coffee. "It was easier, from a financial perspective. It wasn't easy from a personal standpoint. I don't know how long you lived at home once you turned eighteen. For me it was difficult. My mother and aunts are all cut from the same cloth, and they expected me to be the same as them. I'm not, and we argued a lot."

He leaned forward. "How are you different?"

"I want to explore more things, see more places, do more than living here in Portsmouth will allow me. The older generations in my family don't understand."

He smiled. "I started college at eighteen. I went home that first summer and was miserable. My parents wanted to treat me like I was still a young kid, when I'd done a lot of growing up during that year. I never stayed more than a few nights at my parents' house again."

"So you know how I feel. You probably don't know this: my family has a genetic problem. Women almost always give birth to twins, and one of the twins dies very young. Being the surviving twin for my mother makes me extra precious and she's always been overprotective."

"That sounds horrible. Is it the same for your aunts?"

"Yes. Each of my two cousins has a dead sister as well."

He took a sip of coffee and looked at me for a moment, real concern in his eyes. "I hate to be blunt, but why keep having children? It doesn't sound like the pain is worth it," he said.

"Why does anyone have children? Because they want them, regardless of their health or for how long they get to spend with them."

"Do you think you'll have children?" he asked.

I glanced at the tape. "I hardly think that's information you need for the interrogation, do you?"

He laced his fingers behind his head. "No. You're right. I let my curiosity get the better of me. I'm sorry for your family's losses."

I tried to thank him, but I had a lump in my throat and couldn't say anything.

"So, Trina didn't pay you at all, is that right?" he asked, sounding much more official.

"No. She didn't pay me."

"And how did that make you feel?" he asked.

I'd never considered how it made me feel. It was just the way it was. "When I first started working at The Fancy Tart, I was exhausted all the time. I'd never had a job where I had to be in at four or five in the morning, and it was difficult to get used to. Once I gave in and went to bed at nine, it got much better. So I guess I started off resentful, but I haven't felt that way for a while now."

"Nine? That seems early."

"Not to anyone who needs to be awake and happy by five in the morning," I said.

He sat forward and stared into my eyes with a look that had lost all friendliness. "And you were angry at Trina for not paying you, so that you could quit the difficult bakery job."

His change in tone startled me. He said this as though he completely believed it, and like I should believe it as well.

"No. Not at all. I like the bakery job. Now that I'm used to it, I like being up early and seeing the sun rise. I don't miss being up until midnight, wasting my time doing nothing until I'm tired enough to fall asleep. If I'd never taken the bakery job, I'd never have learned these things about myself." I tried not to sound defensive, but I didn't like where this question was leading.

"We have witnesses who put you at the apothecary the night of the murder."

I didn't say anything, because he hadn't asked me a question. Besides, unless they were witnesses who saw me at six in the evening, when Trina was still alive, he was straight-up lying to me. My face flushed as I realized he was lying to see if I would confess.

He waited for me to speak. I took a bite of Danish and a sip of coffee instead. I wouldn't let him frighten me into anything.

Finally, he said, "What do you have to say about that?"

Round one to me. "What time did they see me?" I asked.

"They weren't sure, sometime after ten."

"Your witnesses are mistaken. Or lying. Or not even real. By ten o'clock that night I was in my apartment, fast asleep," I snapped.

He stood and leaned over the table. "You calling me a liar?" he said as his face reddened.

I pulled away from him, afraid of his sudden turn in temper. In my mind, I heard my mother's early training, warning me to keep my temper. I settled my mind and found the truth in the situation. The truth was I was at home, asleep, and he was wrong.

"Like I said, your witnesses are mistaken. I know you don't have to tell me the truth and I think all this time getting coffee and eating pastry was your way of softening me up to trust you."

"My witness isn't lying."

Interesting. Witness, not witnesses. He was definitely lying to me. "Now it's only one witness? They're still wrong."

He sat in his chair, took the legal pad and pencil he had brought into the room and threw it in front of me. "Write down where you were and what you did that night. Include what you used to hit Trina over the head, and why you wanted to kill the woman who had been kind to you."

Had he not been listening to me? Again, I remembered my mother's warning as I felt the tingle of magic rolling across my skin. After a deep, cleansing breath, I realized he had not read

105

me my rights. I wasn't under arrest. I had no obligation to answer any of his questions, much less write out a false confession.

I mustered all my courage and stood. As much as it frightened me to, I stepped close to him and stared him in the eye. "I'll do no such thing. If I'm not under arrest, I'll be going now. If you have any other *reasonable* questions, questions that will lead you to Trina's killer, I'm available."

I walked to the door, hoping it was unlocked, because I was going to look like an idiot if I wasn't able to walk out of there on my own.

The moment my hand touched the knob, it moved, and the door swung open. Relief flooded through me until I saw Chief Dobbins, a harried expression on his face.

Chapter 11

I presume it is all right for me to leave?" I asked.

Chief Dobbins stepped to the side of the interrogation room door. "Of course. You're not under arrest. Before you go, I'd like to talk to you for a few minutes."

I looked at him skeptically. Clearly, I couldn't trust Palmer, so why would I trust him? "I promise you'll be able to leave whenever you want. I'd like to explain a bit about what Detective Palmer was doing."

I supposed it wouldn't kill me to listen to his explanation. After all, he had told me what time Trina died the last time we talked; maybe he would let more information slip.

"Lead the way," I said.

Once he closed the door to his office, he said, "Please sit. Can I get you anything?"

I shook my head as I sat on the arm of the visitor's chair. "Other than my Danish that I left in the interrogation room, no. I'd rather get out of here as quickly as possible."

He sat behind his desk. "I was watching the interview through the one-way mirror. I was probably as surprised as you were when Palmer suddenly changed from chatting to accusing you of murder. I don't require my detectives to discuss their interrogations with me. In this case, I wish he had, because I would have warned him his technique wouldn't work on a Proctor woman."

On a Proctor woman? How well did he know my family?

"I appreciate that. So, tell me, was he telling the truth when he said he had a witness?" I asked.

"As I said, we don't discuss interrogations. Palmer has only been here for a few months. He came here from Boston, and they do things differently there. They assume each suspect is guilty, and then tell them to confess."

"Don't they get a lot of false confessions? I was intimidated in there. A more frightened woman would do whatever it took to get away from that angry man."

The chief rested his arms on his desk. "A

lot fewer than you might imagine. And if a person is going to recant, it will be almost immediately after they get out of the interrogation room. If they wait much longer, we're sure we've got a strong case."

"So all a criminal has to do is be more stubborn than your detective, and they get to walk out?"

The chief laughed. "No, not at all. If we had strong evidence in this case, we'd use it to find her killer."

I didn't like the way that sounded. Railroading confessions through intimidation seemed unnecessary in Portsmouth.

"Isabella. Uh, Miss Proctor, you know I have a long history with your family, and I hope you understand that I hold all the Proctor women, including yourself, in high regard."

I nodded slowly, wondering for the millionth time why the aunts didn't talk about their past.

"I understand why you'd be confused and angry about your interrogation, and I wanted to explain. I'd hate for you to be soured against the idea of joining the force by this one experience," he said.

Time for a little manipulation. "I'm afraid Detective Palmer has already done that for you. My aunts are going to be disappointed with my treatment here."

The chief paled.

I paused for another moment before I continued. "I suppose we could work something out, and I wouldn't have to tell them."

The chief leaned forward. "Go on."

"First, I'd like to know if there was a witness, because their statement is a lie, or at least, they mistook someone else for me. My roommate will tell you I was home and asleep by ten. And second, I'm curious about when you said you had no hard evidence to go on. I mean, aren't there any fingerprints or DNA samples or anything?"

"Palmer hasn't told me about any witnesses."

Aha! Now I knew what Palmer looked like when he was lying. The chief's skin flushed and he tried to bluster his way through being caught by intimidating his witness. This could be helpful in the future.

"Ordinarily, we would have physical evidence on the body or on the premises. We have Trina's fingerprints and assumed yours were the other set we found on the cash register and in the prep room. Understandable, since you worked there. Trina's were on everything too. We found a lot of other prints on the jars, all unique. Unless the store was trashed by a mob, then whoever did it was wearing gloves. There was an oily boot print on a piece of paper, made by size ten men's Timberland steel-toed boots."

Timberland boots were a dime a dozen in New Hampshire. Even factoring in the size, that wasn't much of a clue.

"There was no evidence of the killer on the rock with her blood on it, either," he continued.

Suddenly my head began to spin. I hadn't thought about a murder weapon, or what it might be. I felt stupid and naive, like a little girl who thought she was a grown-up.

"Miss Proctor, are you all right?" The chief called to his secretary for a glass of water. When she handed it to me, I wasn't sure I'd be able to keep it down.

"Take small sips," she said. "I promise you'll feel better."

The first sip roiled around in my stomach but stayed down. I took one more sip and decided not to press my luck with a third.

"I'll get someone to drive you home," the chief said.

"I'd appreciate that."

Getting more information out of him would have to wait. To my horror, he called for Palmer on his intercom and told him to drive me home.

"No, thank you. I can get a cab."

Palmer knocked and walked into the

office. He sat on the edge of the chief's desk and handed me my coffee and Danish. "I'm sorry about the interrogation. Accusations are established procedure in my old department. I didn't think you'd admit to a crime you didn't commit, but if you had an inkling of guilt in you, I could get you to confess."

I stared at him, brows drawn, and magic tingling down my fingers. I needed to calm down, or I was going to cast a spell unintentionally.

"It's a compliment, really," he continued.

"You don't do well with women, do you Detective? 'I don't think I can intimidate you too much' is not the kind of compliment women like to hear," I snapped.

Behind him, the chief snorted. "She's got you there, Steve."

"You're probably right," he said. "Let me make it up to you by driving you home. I promise no interrogation and no intimidation."

It was getting late and I wanted to check in on Grandma again, so I took him up on his offer. Having the police as my personal taxi service seemed like a good use of taxpayer's money right about now.

"Fine. You can bring me to Proctor House instead."

This caught the chief's attention. "You're not going to tell your Aunt Lily about this, are you?"

"Grandma isn't feeling well, I doubt you'll come up." Did I feel bad about lying to him? Not even a little. I absolutely intended to tell them.

"Good. Palmer, I expect you back immediately. We need to adjust your idea of interrogation techniques."

On the way out to the car, Palmer asked, "What's up with you and the chief? I've never seen him take such an interest in one single witness or suspect."

"And which am I? Witness or suspect?"

"You're not a suspect. And you're not a witness, although finding the body does make you involved."

"He has the idea I'm interested in police work and want to join the force. I haven't had the heart to tell him otherwise."

Palmer laughed. "Not with him treating you like a Fabergé egg, that's for sure. What gave him that idea?"

"He mistook my interest in the case for an interest in police work. All I want is to figure out who killed Trina."

Palmer stopped walking. "Don't. It's dangerous, and you don't want to get between a murderer and their escape to freedom. If a person has killed once, they'll kill again to stay free."

I scoffed. "I doubt I'm important enough

for someone to want to kill."

He touched my arm and I looked up at him. I was surprised by the concern in his eyes. "I mean it, Isabella. Call me and I'll take care of it. Promise me."

I didn't want to promise something I had no intention of doing. "I promise I'll call you if I think I'll be in life-threatening danger."

He didn't need to know I could take care of myself, most of the time.

Chapter 12

Palmer and I didn't talk for the short ride to my family's house. The flirtatious banter we'd had on the way to the station was replaced by an awkward silence, broken only by the clicking of the car's turn signal.

When we got to the house, I jumped out of the car. "Thank you for the ride. I appreciate it."

"Remember what you promised. No going after killers."

I waved as I walked toward the house, not willing to repeat my almost lie.

Thea opened the front door when I got to it. "Who was that?"

I rolled my eyes. "Detective Palmer. What a jerk!"

She closed the door behind me. "Since

when do you have handsome guys driving you around? And police detectives, no less?"

I scowled. "You wouldn't care about how he looked, if he accused you of murder."

Thea's eyes widened. "No way! Why would he think that?"

"According to the police chief, it's easier to convince a guilty person to admit their guilt than to do the legwork and find evidence. Since I didn't crack, they decided I'm innocent."

Thea frowned. "Of course they did. You are, right? I mean, they're not questioning you because you did anything wrong, are they?" she asked hesitantly.

I stopped for a moment. Did Thea think I was capable of murder?

"Not that you'd kill anyone, but did you fight with her or something?"

I punched her lightly in the shoulder. "Don't be an idiot." Desperate to change the subject before she returned to how handsome Palmer was, I said, "What's happening today?"

We walked to the kitchen and Delia said, "Trina's funeral is in three days, and we're starting to get ready."

Aunt Nadia turned from the sink to look at me. "Oh, Isabella, you're here. Good. You can start drying the dishes."

The six of us, everyone but Grandma,

worked through the afternoon preparing to feed the people who would come to pay their respects.

Thea sat at the table. "And we have good news. The five of us scoured the house. There was nothing in the bathrooms, or in Grandma's room. We found tea in the kitchen that none of us had tried."

"Grandma got tea in the mail?" I asked as I took the lettuce out of the refrigerator.

"It came a few weeks ago from her friend, Hope, in Sewall," Aunt Nadia said.

Grandma had a lot of friends in witch communities around the world that I'd never met. Sewall was a town further north, hidden from non-witches. Most witches in New Hampshire lived there, because they didn't need to hide their abilities.

"She put it in the cupboard and I forgot all about it. The tea has salvia in it. Salvia! No wonder she thought she was seeing ghosts," Aunt Nadia continued.

I wasn't sure salvia explained Grandma's fatigue. It was a strong hallucinogen and not legal in several states. Why would Hope want to poison Grandma? "How did you know what was in the tea?" I asked. "I mean, you didn't test it on anyone else, right?"

Aunt Nadia pulled a pan of brownies out of the oven. "Of course not. We know a few identification spells. Once your mother tested it and saw it was poisoned, we threw it away. There's no sense in tempting fate by leaving it around."

"Is it still out in the bin?"

Aunt Nadia nodded. "Should be right on the top."

First, Grandma was poisoned, then Trina was murdered. Were the two related? I wasn't sure. One thing I did know is that the police were not ready to deal with anything magic, and they'd need my help. I stepped outside and looked at the driveway. There was still a little snow on the ground, and the plants in the gardens were still dormant. I opened the lid to the trash barrel, took a piece of newspaper from the recycling and picked up the tin of tea. If there was any salvia on the outside of the container, I didn't want it on me. I opened the tin and took a gentle sniff. Citrus blend.

I closed my eyes and focused on the tea and its ingredients. This process wasn't nearly as mystical as it sounded. It was like trying to pick out all the instruments in a piece of music, only with food or drink. When I first learned how to do this, food tasted disgusting to me because I tasted the individual ingredients—flour, egg, salt, whatever—and I wasn't tasting the combination. It took three weeks for me to learn to turn the ability on and off before I could eat anything that wasn't a one-ingredient food. Now I kept it turned off unless I really needed it.

Aunt Nadia was right. The tea had salvia in it. I'd learned a bit about it at the apothecary, and it was not something we carried. One of the problems was that it was contraindicated in diets that included many common foods, like lemon and garlic. And the potion I made for Grandma had lemon in it. No wonder she had such a strong reaction.

I tossed the tea in the trash and closed the lid. Grandma would deal with Hope when she was ready. For now, I needed to figure out how, using my intuition, I had made a potion for Grandma that harmed her. I could have killed my own grandma, and I might have, if she hadn't freaked out in the restaurant.

My chest tightened as guilt overwhelmed me. I sank to the stairs by the trash barrel and sat with my head in my hands. I didn't want to think about this, and I didn't want to go into the house and confront my family. They must know this was all my fault. And if there was any lasting damage to Grandma, I'd never forgive myself.

Clearly, I wasn't ready to make potions on my own, and I certainly wasn't ready to run the apothecary. I hoped Trina left it to someone more qualified; maybe a witch from Sewall. I would be a temporary manager for them until they found someone else to run the store. Then I'd leave, work at the bakery, and lead a life without magic. I shouldn't be trusted with any more responsibility than that.

I was shivering by the time my mother came outside.

"I thought I'd find you out here," she said.

I turned my head away from her and burst into tears.

She sat next to me on the steps and wrapped an arm around my shoulders. "There was no way to prevent this."

I sniffled. "But I . . . but I . . .,"

"Listen to me. There was no way you could know your grandmother was being poisoned when you made your potion. No one could have. Not me, not Trina, no one. No more of this holding yourself responsible for something that wasn't your fault. This is why you never, ever make a potion for a person that you have not seen recently. To be safe, they should be right in front of you."

"It was my fault," I whispered.

"No. It wasn't. It's the fault of the person who wanted to kill your grandmother. Even without your potion, she would have died in the next few months and we would have believed it was from natural causes."

Leaf of Faith

"But—"

"No buts." She shivered. "Let's go inside. I'll make you a cup of cocoa to warm up, and we'll talk more."

When I didn't answer or move, she snapped at me. "Do as I tell you, Isabella."

At twenty-one years old, I still wasn't immune from the "mom voice," so I got up and followed her to the kitchen. Besides, her hot cocoa was delicious.

She busied herself making cocoa while I sat at the table. "You need to change your perspective. If you hadn't given the potion to Grandma, we would never have found the poison. You saved her."

As if to underscore what she said, Grandma walked into the kitchen. She had color back in her cheeks, and her eyes were bright and clear. "There's my smart girl."

I gave her a weak smile. "I'm not feeling smart right now. I might be a little lucky."

Grandma sat next to me at the table. "Piffle. You made exactly what I needed to get well. I've got to tell you that I feel better now than I have in weeks. Don't be a fool and beat yourself up over this."

My mother set a mug of cocoa in front of me. I blew on it, but knew it was too hot to drink yet.

"I made you hallucinate," I said.

Grandma pursed her lips. "That'll be enough of this self-indulgent claptrap from you, young lady. I am up and healthy because of your actions. Hope is the one who has to answer for this, not you."

She took a sip of my cocoa. "If Trina were still alive, what would she say"?

"That's easy. She'd tell me not to blame myself when things go right. I should take the win and learn from the experience," I said, not believing what I was saying.

"Exactly right," said Grandma.

I sat quietly for a minute and watched Grandma drink my cocoa. She seemed to feel much better. No hallucinations, no talking to imaginary friends. Relief washed through me as I put my arm around her and gave her a squeeze.

At five, Aunt Nadia handed me the bread dough that had been in the fridge.

I looked at Grandma. "How did you make this?"

She smiled. "Once your mother and aunts cast a purifying spell on me, I felt much better."

"I'm relieved. We were worried about you," I said.

"Takes more than a little poison to put me out of commission. Not having rolls for dinner is going to make me cranky, and no one wants that.

Get to work."

I kissed her cheek and did as she said.

Once we got to the dinner table, the seven of us talked about how much better Grandma felt. Each of my family members made a point to say that if I hadn't brought the potion, she might be dead by now. By the time they got around to toasting me, I had to put a stop to it.

"Detective Palmer questioned me today," I said in a desperate attempt to get them to stop praising me.

Aunt Lily put her wine glass down, waiting for me to continue. If I wasn't careful, the chief was going to get an earful from her tomorrow morning.

"Why?" my mother asked. "They already questioned you." Her voice got louder and higher. "You're not a suspect, are you? Because if you are, I'll march right down there and give Dobbins a piece of my mind."

How to explain this in a way that told the whole truth and kept the chief out of too much trouble? "No, Mom, it's not necessary. The police needed to ask some follow-up questions, and I wanted to help. I want Trina's killer found as much as anyone else, so I was glad they got me off their list of suspects."

"You were a suspect?" Delia asked. "Trina's always been good to you. Did you tell them that? Did you tell them she's family?"

Chatter erupted around the table, and I had to speak louder to be heard. "Hey! It's okay. We all have the same goal here. Let's not freak out about what the police are doing. They're following the usual pattern of questioning people closest to the victim, and it's natural they wanted to talk to me early on."

My grandmother was still muttering about Dobbins, even though the rest of the table was quiet.

"Now, let me tell you what I've learned," I said.

That even got Grandma to be quiet.

"Unfortunately, not much. Trina was killed at about one thirty in the morning. The killer left no physical evidence outside and only one clear boot print in the office. The shop was trashed after she was killed, and her killer destroyed almost everything in a rage."

Aunt Lily scoffed. "Of course the killer was angry. You don't kill people out of joy, do you?"

"I mean angrier than usual, I guess. That's the impression Detective Palmer gave me."

"Is he the one who dropped you off?" Delia asked.

Apparently, Thea had blabbed. I rolled my eyes. "Yes. He's the one who questioned me, and to make up for being such a jerk, he drove me here.

Trust me, he's not done making up for the questioning."

My mother's eyes went icy with anger, and before she said anything, my phone rang.

"Hi, Isabella. It's Detective Palmer."

"Good evening, Detective. How can I help you?" I said loudly enough for everyone at the table to hear me as I walked into the hall.

"I wanted to tell you that the scene—I mean, the apothecary is almost done being processed and you can go in tomorrow morning."

"Good. Thanks. I can clean everything up then?"

"Yes. We're done. Although, if you find anything missing or suspicious, I would appreciate a call. I'm sure you want to help us in any way you can."

I frowned. I wasn't as excited about helping them as I was about finding the killer myself. If the murderer was another witch, the police could be in danger they couldn't protect themselves from. "If anything comes to mind, I'll call. But if your idea of helping involves more questioning like today, I'm not interested."

He sighed. "About that. Believe me, I'm in enough trouble for today's interrogation from Chief Dobbins. I don't need more trouble, so I'm treating you—your whole family—with kid gloves from now on."

I felt a little bad for him. "Why? What did he say?"

"The chief told me in no uncertain terms that you and your family would never kill anyone."

"He's right. He didn't say why, did he?"

"No. In fact, I was going to ask you the same question. Why does your family get a pass from scrutiny?"

I had no idea. I'm sure Aunt Lily could tell him, but so far, her lips were sealed.

"Miss Proctor?" he prompted when I didn't say anything.

"Oh, sorry. I was thinking about your question. You'd have to ask the chief about that."

"Make sure you call if you find something we've missed," he said before he hung up.

I returned to the dining room to find my family at the door, trying to listen to my conversation.

"The shop is ready to be opened tomorrow. I'm going to have to go in and clean it all up."

"All of it?" my mother asked. "The place was trashed. You'll have to throw everything out and start fresh."

I cringed at the idea. "Yes, I will. Cleaning will give me time to find any clues the police missed."

Leaf of Faith

Any clues they would have missed would be magic-related, and the police weren't prepared to deal with a paranormal murderer. For as much as Palmer thought he was protecting me, I was also protecting him.

Chapter 13

I woke up early, or at least earlier than I would have for a day I wasn't going into the bakery. Six o'clock in the morning still felt like a luxury to me. I dressed in my worst clothes, ready to get incredibly dirty while cleaning out the apothecary.

The storm Mrs. Thompson predicted had left five inches of heavy snow, turning Portsmouth into a fairy wonderland. Plows had been working through the night, so roads and sidewalks were already cleared off. By the time I got to the

I stopped by The Fancy Tart for breakfast and a mid-morning snack, and to check in with Bethany. I had to cut my hours for the next week to get the apothecary set up for whoever inherited the business. It probably wasn't my responsibility, but I couldn't stand the idea of Trina's life's work in shambles, and there was no way I would leave our customers stranded.

Omar greeted me and immediately turned to make me a drink. He handed me a Sumatra coffee. "You need this. And don't squawk at the sugar in it. If you saw how bad you looked, you'd thank me."

I tried to smile and took the coffee. The truth was, he was right. This morning I hadn't liked what I saw in the mirror. I had deep bags under my eyes and I couldn't bring myself to smile. How an extra packet or two of sugar was going to fix this, I didn't know, but it was nice that he was trying to cheer me up. The warm cup thawed my cold fingers and the aroma of the coffee made my mouth water.

"Can I get an egg and cheese on an English muffin and an éclair?" I asked.

He raised an eyebrow. "Which are you eating first?"

"The egg and cheese. The éclair is for later."

He relayed my sandwich order to the kitchen and bagged up the éclair for me. "How are you?"

"The police have released the apothecary and I'm going in to clean it."

"I heard it was basically destroyed inside. That's a lot to do."

"Yeah, well, there's no one else to do it. Trina didn't have much close family. Her ex-husband isn't reliable, and neither is her nephew. I don't think the shop is destroyed. All the stock will need to be replaced, though. The thing I'm going to hate to clean most is the greenhouse. The plants died, and Trina and I put a lot of work into growing them. It's like losing a pet, only there were hundreds of plants in there." I frowned at this thought. So much work ruined because someone was angry. It was senseless.

"I'm sorry you have to do all that." He handed me my order. "It's on the house."

I suspected the minute I got into the kitchen he'd pay for my meal himself and made a mental note to do something nice for him when I got this whole mess sorted out.

In the kitchen, Bethany looked up from the giant mixer she was adding flour to. "Oh, I didn't expect to see you today."

"I'm not on the schedule. I wanted to talk to you about working fewer hours this week. The police have released the apothecary, and I need to clean it up and get it running again."

She turned the mixer off and wiped her hands on her apron. "You're going to keep it running?"

"Yes. I'll at least try to keep our regular customers supplied until whoever inherits the business can take over."

"Stop by tonight and I'll have a revised schedule drawn up. Call me if I can help you with anything else."

I smiled and thanked her before I headed out to erase the signs of Trina's murder and pretend I wasn't on the verge of tears. I wasn't fooling myself, and I doubted I'd fool any customers who stopped by.

Knowing the lingering smell of alcohol in the apothecary would ruin my appetite, I ate my breakfast on the short walk over.

I left my coffee and éclair by the back door of the apothecary and tackled the greenhouse first. I unlocked the door and stepped inside. The smell of alcohol had dissipated over the past few days, and all I saw were dead plants. I took them out, one by one, throwing them in the dumpster. I didn't bother to save the small plastic pots. I kept the clay pots for replanting, even though it would be many months before the new plants I bought would require it.

With each trip to the dumpster, I passed the bushes I found Trina behind. After a half an hour, I'd gotten used to walking back and forth in front of the spot, and I stopped shuddering.

I was working fast, trying to get through the cleaning as quickly as possible.

"Isabella, we've come to help," my mother

said.

My entire family stood at the end of the alley, dressed in work clothes with gloves and boots, and I burst into tears. I hadn't realized how upset being alone with this job made me, and how much of a burden it felt.

My mother rushed over to me. "You never have to go it alone in life, honey. You've always got family."

My aunts, cousins, and grandmother joined her in a group hug and wouldn't let go until I stopped crying.

"You've made a good start. Why don't you all keep going with the plants. I'll inspect the crime scene," Grandma said.

I gave quick instructions to save the clay pots and then joined Grandma outside by the bushes. "What are you looking for?"

"The police aren't that smart. They can miss a lot, and if there was any witchy business going on, I may be able to feel it."

My cousins and I had tried the same thing when we were here two nights ago, to no avail. Grandma, though, was better at everything than we were. If there was something to be discovered, I was sure she'd feel it.

"Trina was killed over there," I said, pointing to the patch of ground that had all the gravel scooped away.

Leaf of Faith

Grandma moved to the center of the patch and closed her eyes. It didn't take any weird hand gestures or magic wands for her to pull up her power. She stood there, opened herself up to the universe and listened.

She stood still for ten minutes. I got bored watching her, because I couldn't feel what she was feeling. I went to help with the greenhouse and was surprised what five extra people accomplished in such a short time. The greenhouse was almost halfway emptied.

I grabbed a large pot and was about to bring it outside when Delia said, "Isabella, look!" She pointed to a small rosemary plant that was still green. "It's still alive."

"How did that happen?" I asked.

"It was hiding behind this larger plant, and the jerk who did all this must have missed it."

I picked the plant up and hugged it to my chest. Sappy and sentimental, but it felt right. Knowing something survived this nightmare gave me hope. "I'm going to bring it into the shop."

Grandma was still doing her thing, so I left her alone. I fished in my pocket for the keys to the store and then opened the door. The stench of alcohol and rot assaulted my nose. All the potions and ingredients had spent the last couple days mingling into one giant, putrid smell I didn't want to breathe.

I set the plant down next to the cash register, skirted around most of the mess on the floor and opened the front window. I turned around and inspected the shop. Fingerprint powder covered the flat surfaces, giving the normally bright and sunny sales floor a gloomy feel. It was a good thing my family was here, or this would have taken a week to fully clean.

In the quiet, I could hear the voicemail beeping. I walked back to the office and pressed the button to listen to the messages.

"This is Hanson's Cleaning. We are sorry for your loss and wanted to extend our services to you in this sad time. We are available for all your crime scene–related cleaning needs. Please call to discuss how we can help you."

Wow. I had no idea cleaners were now ambulance chasers too. I deleted the message and moved on to the next one.

"Just because Trina's gone doesn't mean I don't expect to get my money back. Talk to Frank and get this sorted out."

My heart raced. I didn't recognize the man's voice, and I didn't have that much money. I saved the message and would tell Detective Palmer about it the next time I saw him.

I closed the office door before anyone came in. I wanted to be the one to go through all the papers and see if there were any clues the police had missed.

When I went back outside, Grandma was ordering everyone around and not actually doing any work herself.

"Feel anything?" I asked.

She shook her head. "This was the most mundane murder I've ever felt. No magic to it whatsoever. Not even magical defense, which means Trina didn't know she was in danger."

There was no reason to assume it was a witch-related murder then. Maybe her death was a random act of violence.

"I'm going to go inside and organize the office," I said.

"You might want these," said Thea as she handed me my coffee and éclair.

"Thanks. I'm sure I will."

I opened the door to the office and surveyed the mess. I wasn't sure where to begin. I wouldn't be able to tell what was missing until the office was organized. I tackled the desk first, inspecting each drawer before I put it back in the desk. I felt along the inside of the desk for anything taped and hiding. I found nothing. Refiling the paperwork was an eye-opening experience for me. The business was doing quite well, financially speaking, even though there was never much money in the bank. Did Trina not deposit all the money she brought in? Where did the money go? How much was Frank taking from her?

I made a list of all our suppliers. We didn't have many since we started growing our own plants. I'd have to get in touch with them and reorder as much as I could afford.

At some point, my family had come in and started cleaning the sales area. It was nice to have them with me, laughing and keeping spirits up in the face of such an ugly mess.

I was almost done with the loose papers when I found an empty folder marked "Experimental." Nothing I had filed away seemed like it should go in this folder, so I set it on the cleared-off desktop. What would have gone in here? Trina told me she stuck to the old recipes, the old knowledge. She said she wasn't an experimentalist, and that she knew of too many people who were hurt by potions gone wrong.

Still . . . what had been in this folder?

I finished putting away the papers and then turned to the old, leatherbound books that had filled Trina's bookshelves. I flipped through each one, searching for notes or missing pages. *Drostov's Book of Potions and the Healing Arts* had the entire section on love potions ripped out.

We never made love potions, infinite purses, or any other thing like that. I checked the infinite purse section, and it was intact. Was Trina killed for a love potion, or had she removed this section herself? Her death didn't seem like a random murder anymore.

I took the book out to the sales counter and was amazed at how much work had been done.

"Wow!" I exclaimed. The floor was clean and washed, the entire store was devoid of fingerprint powder, and the aunts had restocked the shelves with anything still left in the prep room. "I can't believe how much you've done. You've been working hard."

"We've been here for hours," Thea said.

I peeked at my watch. It was noon already, and I had no idea time had flown by that quickly. My mother and grandmother were rearranging what little merchandise we could still sell, and my Aunt Lily was washing the windows.

"Let me buy you lunch," I said. "It's the least I can do."

"Can't, we've got lunch cooking at home. Why don't you come home instead?" Aunt Nadia said.

I was about to say yes when Mrs. Thompson knocked on the door. Reluctantly, I opened the door for her.

"Are you open?" she asked, scanning the mostly bare shelves.

"Not officially. But since you're here, how can I help?"

She patted my arm. "Thank you, dear. I need more of the kidney tonic for Jameson. Can you make that?"

I pulled out the formulary of current patients and found Jameson's page. I didn't have the licorice root his potion needed in stock. "I can't make this for you now. I can drop some off tonight," I told her. I knew with the recipe in the formulary I would make no mistakes in the potion.

"Thank you, dear. He's not as chipper as usual," she said.

As she left the store, the letter carrier came in. "Good to see you're open," she said. "My sciatica is kicking up again, and I need some more of that turmeric solution. Do you have any?"

"Just a second," I said as I peeked in the prep room. It was also organized and swept. My family could get a lot done if they put their minds to it.

"Nope, we're out. We're out of most things right now. I'll call when I get a new shipment."

She frowned. "I guess that'll have to do. I held your mail for the last couple days. Here it is," she said, handing me a thick wad of envelopes.

I took the mail. "I suggest some gentle yoga and a soak in the tub with Epsom salts. I'm ordering supplies later on today, and I'll make sure yours are on the list. Eat a garlicky meal tonight too."

"Epsom salts? I'll pick some up on my way home. As for yoga, every time I try, I wind up falling over on the living room floor, and my kids laugh at me."

I smiled. The first couple weeks I did yoga the same thing happened to me. "I know that feeling. Keep at it and you'll get better. I did."

After she left, Aunt Lily turned to me. "You're a natural here. The new owners would do well to hire you, and not as an apprentice."

One great thing about my family was I could always trust what they said. Sure, they were supportive and loving, but compliments had to be earned. If Aunt Lily said I was good at something, then I was. I beamed at her. "Thanks, auntie. I hope they will, too."

I was surprised to see they had finished. They must have used a few spells when no one was looking. "I guess we're done cleaning up here. I'm not sure what to do next."

"Next, you flip the sign on the door to "Open" and you let customers in," said Aunt Nadia. "We're going to get out of your way. Come over for dinner tonight?"

My family loved me, and I knew they were upset that I had moved out. Every dinner lately had been another excuse for my mom to pressure me to move home. I didn't have the energy to deal with that. Going home shouldn't bring up visions of the General Ackbar "It's a trap!" meme. "Maybe tomorrow night," I said.

"Okay. You come tomorrow and I'll make something special," she said.

Once they left, I turned the sign and unlocked the door. I finished taking inventory and tried to find some potions I could make, with no success.

The mail was the usual bills and flyers, and an envelope addressed to me in Trina's handwriting. Tears welled in my eyes, and I set it down. She'd never written to me before. With a steadying breath, I opened the envelope.

Dear Isabella,

This is not the first letter I've written to you when I felt my life was in danger. I hope I can throw it away like all the others I've written. This time, though, I can feel the hand of death around my heart, and I fear it won't let go.

You were right to question me about the phone call and the person you assumed was an angry customer. It was my ex-husband. It pains me to say that he is in deep financial trouble and the amount of money I am able to spare from the business each month is no longer enough. If I can't keep him afloat, then I'm not sure what he'll do.

I started this business when we were still married, but he thinks that since we're divorced, I need to repay him all the money we invested to get the apothecary up and running.

He's not the only person I'm worried about. Caroline Arneson is threatening legal action. For years, she's wanted to expand her business into our space, but I was unwilling to give up the lease. Over the past six months she's become quite insistent.

My nephew, James, isn't of the highest integrity. He used to work for me, and right before you became my apprentice, I fired him for stealing from the till. He's angry at me, and you. Be careful around him. He thinks he deserves the shop, even though he has no magical ability at all.

Finally, there are customers who are angry because I won't give them the potions they want. You know the type of potions I mean. There's a stronger presence of evil in town lately and we must all guard against that. In a desperate attempt to get them off my back, I have experimented with potions that will give them what they want at a heavy cost. The potions will leave them worse than before they took them. I haven't used any yet. You can find them in the experimental folder in the office.

Use them only in a dire emergency, and never use them on yourself.

You have been a joy to teach, Isabella, and I have faith that you will succeed in life through your determination, compassion, and wit.

I hope you never have to read this,

Lisa Bouchard

Trina

Chapter 14

I got to work at seven thirty the next morning, ready to tackle the day and make Trina proud. I knew I'd miss her presence for a long time to come but focusing on her memory helped ease my loneliness. I was pleased to find deliveries waiting for me, propped up against the back door. I did my best not to look at the bushes by the greenhouse as I picked up the packages and brought them into the prep room.

Over half the orders I'd placed yesterday were already here, and I'd be able to get a lot of potions made today. I pulled out the ingredients I'd need and got to work. When my alarm rang at ten to unlock the door, I was pleased to see a few people waiting outside.

"Good morning, everyone. As you can see,

there's not a lot of stock on the shelves, and there's nothing in the greenhouse. I'm doing my best to restock all the supplies, although it may take a little time. I'm also working on filling orders as quickly as possible for all our loyal customers. If I don't have what you need, I'll be happy to take your order and make it as soon as I can."

"Our" loyal customers—who was I talking about? I was alone there, though it felt wrong to say *my* loyal customers. It would take a while before they felt like they were mine.

Mrs. Thompson was the first to approach the counter.

"What can I get for you today?"

"Nothing for me, dear. I have something you might like." She reached into her purse and pulled out a photo of Trina in a simple silver frame, smiling in the sun.

I took the picture, remembering the joy Trina took in spending sunny days outside. "Thank you. When was this taken?"

"Last year at Market Square Day. She had a booth out at Prescott Park and had the time of her life."

She had, too. Her wide smile was a contrast to the more controlled smiles she used over the past several months.

"She seems happier than I've seen in a long time," I said.

"I thought you'd want to have her photo here as a tribute to her," Mrs. Thompson said.

"How thoughtful of you. I'm sure Trina would feel honored by how much you cared for her. Do you have an idea about where to put it?" I asked.

"I did. I thought we could put it on the counter. It would be nice to have a candle lit, to give it a memorial feel."

"What a lovely idea," I said.

I placed the photo on the counter and took a white taper in a short silver candlestick holder and set it next to the photo. I rummaged around the drawer for matches, but there weren't any.

"You don't happen to have any matches, do you?" I asked.

Mrs. Thompson smiled and took a small box of matches out of her purse. She pulled one out, and it caught fire without striking the box. My eyes widened, amazed at what Mrs. Thompson had shown me. She was a witch. More than that, she was a witch in town that my family didn't know about, and that was rare.

She lit the candle and blew out the match. "Stop by some time and we can talk."

I was dumbfounded and afraid to say anything. She stepped out of line and I turned to greet the next customer. Only she wasn't there to buy anything.

Caroline Arneson drew herself up to her full height. Her over-teased blonde hair and three-inch heels brought her to five feet four inches, if she was lucky. "Are you the new proprietor here?"

Other people in line stopped talking and stared at us.

"No," I said.

"Then who is paying you? Why are you open?"

I plastered a fake smile on my face, knowing she wanted this space. "It seemed like the right thing to do. I feel an obligation to the customers of this shop, because we provide a vital service to the community. And as you can see, they think so too. Can I get you anything? If not, I'll take the next person in line."

I didn't want her to make trouble on my first solo day, and I hoped she'd leave quickly.

Instead, she turned to face everyone else in the store. "Buy what you can, because this business won't be here much longer. Arneson's Dry Goods will be expanding here soon."

She turned to me. "You're out. One way or another. Pack up your dried flowers and dead leaves and go away."

She had been trying to expand into the apothecary's space for years now, and I wasn't worried by her threats. With my smile never faltering, I said, "You'll have to take that up with

146

the new owner. Good day and thank you for stopping by."

Polite to the last. Trina and my mother would be proud of me for not stooping to her rude level.

Next in line was Mr. Schmidt, asking about a hair tonic. He was a tall, thin man who, despite being in his eighties, had a head of thick, white hair. His formulary page told me I had the ingredients, and it would be ready in two days.

"Don't you listen to Caroline. She's bitter because no one wants to buy her cheap tourist junk, and no amount of extra space is going to change that."

I grinned at Mr. Schmidt. I'd never understood the appeal of her stuff, either. "Come back in two days, and it will be ready for you," I told him.

By eleven, I'd finished with the steady stream of customers and needed a break. I stepped out back to bring in more deliveries, but only had time to set them down in the prep room before the door rang.

A man in a grey suit walked in and set his briefcase down on the back counter. I'd never met him before, but his cheap suit and slicked-back hair screamed cheap lawyer. "Good morning. Can I help you?"

He opened his briefcase and removed a

thick file of papers. "Are you the owner?"

"The former owner passed away recently and her will hasn't been read yet, if she even has one," I replied.

"I see. I'm George Fiske, and I represent Arneson Enterprises. I have some legal documents to serve to the owner of this establishment."

That seemed like a *him* problem. "You'll have to go to the will reading to find out who to serve them to. Until then, I guess you're out of luck."

He scowled. "I don't like your tone, young lady. Who is your boss here?"

Trina had been dead for just a couple days, and already Caroline Arneson was ready to pounce. I didn't feel like I needed to be overly polite to this guy. "I've already answered that question. There's no one here but me. I suppose right now there is no boss, so you can take your papers and . . ."

I'd been doing such a good job being polite to Caroline earlier that I stopped there and let him imagine what I was going to say. At least I couldn't get in trouble for what he thought I might say.

"Why are you working, then? I don't understand. This business shouldn't be open."

I tried to exhale the aggravation he was causing me. "Well, you see, some businesses provide a positive service to the community and strive to help others. Helping people is often its own reward. I am here to honor the memory of my dear friend and mentor and continue to serve our customers. I guess lawyers don't do that sort of thing?"

His face turned red and he turned and walked out.

I had to take a stand. It didn't matter how long I was going to run this business; I couldn't let Caroline try to bully me out of it. I locked the door to my shop and walked next door to hers.

Caroline Arneson was talking in a corner of her shop to Fiske when I walked in, completely ignoring several people waiting at the register. Having more space wasn't going to make up for that kind of bad customer service.

I walked up to them. "Talking about me?"

She had the grace to look a bit sheepish before her attorney took over. "This is a privileged conversation. Please leave."

Now, I didn't know much about attorney/client privilege, but if they were talking in front of strangers, it couldn't be a secret.

I took a step back and surveyed her sales area. She sold the tackiest of tourist memorabilia, and always had. Nothing in her store cost more than about eight dollars; nothing was worth more than about two. I picked up a beach towel with

"Portsmouth" woven into it. It was a thin weave, and I saw light through it when I held it up to the window. Some poor tourist was going to want to dry off with it, only to find it wouldn't absorb any water.

I moved on to the wall of keychains. Yes, an entire wall of lobsters, bridges, state symbols and beach goers. Apparently, they sold well enough. Why else would she devote fifteen feet of floor-to-ceiling space to them?

As I was inspecting them, her lawyer left and she snapped, "Paying customers only," while she rang up the few people in line.

I picked up a lobster keychain as though I was going to buy it and waited for everyone else to leave.

"What do you want?" she asked as the door closed behind the last customer.

"I want you to get off my case. The apothecary isn't moving right now — it can't. Give it a rest until the will is read," I said.

She frowned. "You can sign the property over to me as the de facto owner — you're the only one taking responsibility right now."

That definitely didn't sound true, and there was no way I wanted the kind of trouble that comes with signing legal documents I shouldn't be. "Listen, I'm sure you can work this out with the new owner. I just don't want you coming in and disturbing my business."

She didn't respond, so I assumed she was making things up to get her way.

I set the cheap keychain on the counter. "You know, you have a strong motive for killing Trina. You've been hounding Trina to move for years, and now that she's gone, it's the first real chance you've had to make it happen. You've already harassed her so much she thought about getting the police involved."

Her eyes squinted. "You think I killed her? Don't be foolish."

I smiled at her discomfort. "Well, the police look for a few things, don't they? Means, motive, and opportunity. I just explained your motive. Opportunity is easy with the shared courtyard, and as for means — anyone could have picked up that rock in a fit of anger." She paled as I continued. "Unless, that is, you have an alibi?"

"I . . . I do have one," she stuttered. "I was at the Junior League charity auction. There were at least a hundred people there who saw me."

Junior League — probably something super-boring where everyone drank too much mediocre wine and bid on things they didn't want, just to impress others. I rolled my eyes at the idea.

"Who was at your table?" I asked.

She bit her lip. "I started the night sitting with Mark Goodwin, John and Clara Post, and

Elizabeth Childress."

"What happened to them?"

She grew indignant as she spoke. "I thought these people were my best friends, I guess not. We were all having a wonderful time before the auction, and then they drifted away from the table and joined others instead. They squeezed into other tables rather than sit with me," she pouted.

That seemed strange and not nearly as proper as I imagined these sorts of events were. "Why?"

"It's not like I was drinking much more than the rest of them," she said defensively.

"After they left, you were sitting alone? It sounds like you could have left for a bit and then returned. No one would have noticed."

She shook her head. "I bid heavily on a few auctions and I'm sure there's a record of the one I won. That should clear my name."

There was no chance I'd be able to get a look at that list. The amounts donated to charity didn't seem like something that would be public information. This was going to have to go to Detective Palmer. "I'm sure the police can clear your name."

She grabbed my arm. "Please, no. Don't go to the police."

I raised an eyebrow but didn't say

anything, waiting for her to continue.

"My husband is a sergeant in the Portsmouth PD, and if he got wind of how much I had drunk, and how I behaved, well, he'd be upset with me."

Things had gotten grim, fast. With forty percent of police families reporting domestic violence and more that don't report it, Caroline might be in danger.

"If you can prove to me that you were there and didn't kill Trina, I'll let it drop."

Her eyes teared up. "Can I trust you to keep my secret?"

That was a loaded question. "If you're not going to confess to another crime to get out of this one, then probably."

She squeezed my arm harder. "You have to promise me that you'll keep this between us. I wasn't breaking any laws."

My heart was racing. Was I confronting Trina's killer? I had to see her alibi to know. "Okay, fine. If you're lying to me, I swear I'll set my grandmother on you."

She blanched. "I'm not. I promise." She went to the computer behind her sales counter and pulled up her email. "This video came this morning. My husband will go through the roof if he sees it."

She clicked play and I watched her

hanging over a much younger man. She was drunk and kept trying to kiss him. The poor guy was mortified and doing his best to maintain both their dignities. It was a short clip, and the clock in the background had clearly read 12:02.

"Who's the guy?" I asked.

"He's one of the bachelors that were auctioned off. I'm pretty sure I won him."

I looked closer at his face but didn't recognize him. "You bought a guy at the auction? Yeah, I'm sure no husband would be happy about that. And isn't that illegal?"

"I bought a dinner date with him, that's all. And I have to pay for dinner."

"Who took the video?"

"I wish I knew. I tried to email them back, but it bounced. They want a hundred thousand dollars to erase all copies of it."

I let out a low whistle. "That's a lot of money. Do you have it?"

She shook her head. "My husband would notice if that much money was missing."

I was torn. On the one hand, this woman had been mean to me and Trina for a long time. On the other hand, she was afraid of her husband and had made a bad mistake while drinking. If he found out, I wouldn't be surprised if he took his anger out on her. "I don't know what to say."

"If you don't say anything about the video

or bring me up as a suspect, I'll never bother you or the apothecary again."

What a mess. My suspect was an abused woman, and now I had to keep her secret. Business was one thing, but you don't leave a woman in danger. "Do you promise?"

"This isn't the first time I will have upset my husband, and I can get around most of his anger."

I felt helpless and weak. "I don't like leaving you like this. If I can do anything for you, please call." I wrote my number down for her. "I'm serious. Take care."

I walked to my own shop, worried for her and no closer to finding Trina's killer.

Trina's ex-husband, Frank, was waiting for me in front of the door. I wanted to give him a hug and tell him how sorry I was for his loss, but he looked angry. I unlocked the door and we both walked in.

"Frank, I'm sorry," I said.

"Thanks. You're running the place?"

"I am, since there is no one else who can. It's unofficial. My plan is to help the new owner and keep my job, if I can."

"In that case, maybe we can work out an arrangement."

"Sure, what do you need?"

He walked to the counter. "I loaned Trina

the money to open this shop, and she's been paying me back on a weekly basis. I'd like to keep that payment plan going. I can't wait for everything to be settled with the will."

This wasn't how Trina described their arrangement in her letter. Was he trying to get even more out of me than he was getting from Trina? I needed to stall him. "Oh, ah, sure. Well, at least I think that's okay. I'll have to take a look at the books and see what I can afford. We lost a lot of stock in the break-in, and I need to replace it if I want to keep the customers happy."

I really had to talk to someone about money. Paying for some stock out of my own savings was one thing, but there was no way I could give Frank money.

Frank knocked on the counter with his knuckles. "I'll be back in a couple days, and I expect the full thousand. Trina stopped paying, and you saw what happened to her."

My eyes widened and my heart raced. I nodded, too afraid to say anything.

"I'll see you on soon."

I reached for the stool and sat down. Had he threatened me? Had he confessed to killing Trina?

Chapter 15

As soon as Frank left, I dialed Detective Palmer's cell phone. My hands shook, and I had to dial twice before I got the right number.

Palmer answered with, "Hey, Isabella. Can I call you back? I'm right in the middle of something."

Not even a hello. He must be busy. I almost said yes, but there was no way I'd be able to sleep if I didn't tell him about Frank's threat. At least he could tell me if it was something to worry about or not. "Frank, Trina's ex-husband, threatened me over money and I'm worried he's going to hurt me."

The distracted tone in his voice vanished. "Is he there with you now?"

"No. I'm alone."

"Okay. Stay where you are. Lock the doors and window and I'll be there in three minutes. Don't let anyone in until I get there."

I nodded, although it didn't matter that I hadn't answered him, because he hung up on me. I locked the front and back doors, turned off the lights, and sat under the desk in the office, hugging my knees to my chest and telling myself Palmer would be here any second. His immediate reaction made me realize I should have taken the threat more seriously.

It wasn't long before I heard banging at the front door and Palmer's voice calling my name. I rolled my shoulders to release the tension I held since I hung up the phone, crawled out from under the desk, and opened the door.

"Are you still alone?" he asked.

My lip quivered as I nodded.

He put his arm around my shoulder and pulled me to him. "I've got someone checking out the back of the building, and we've got a BOLO out on Frank. You're safe now, and you don't need to worry."

His reassurance was all I needed to let my guard down fully, and the tears flowed. I hated it when I got all weak like that. My cousins and I had taken years of self-defense classes, and I thought I could defend myself reasonably well, though I'd never had to. I rubbed my eyes and tried to calm my mind. "Thank you. I feel much better now."

"I'll need to take a statement. Is there somewhere we can sit and talk?" he asked.

I led him to the office, and we sat in the visitors' chairs. I still wasn't comfortable using Trina's chair.

Palmer pulled out a notepad. "Take your time, and tell me what happened in as much detail as possible."

I explained the threat and how I had no idea where I was going to get a thousand dollars a week. It was at that point I broke down again. I didn't want to die like Trina.

He handed me a tissue from the desk. "You don't have to pay the money. You don't owe it to him, her estate does, and I'm sure something can be worked out. Trina may have had an agreement with him, but you don't. With a threat like that, I suggest you get a restraining order so he'll have to stay away from you."

I finished drying my tears and blew my nose. I took a deep breath and tried to sit up straighter. Palmer was right. I didn't even own the shop, and there was no way to force me to pay him. If I did wind up inheriting it, then he and I might come to some sort of arrangement, an arrangement I could afford, and it would have to be done through our lawyers. The thought of bringing lawyers into the deal might drive him away.

The door chimes rang, and I froze. Palmer eased his gun from its holster and stood up.

"Detective? It's Kate," a woman's voice called out.

Palmer holstered his gun and walked out of the office. "Anything?"

I followed him onto the sales floor, where a woman about my age in a patrol uniform waited for us. Her long, dark hair was in a severe bun at the nape of her neck. There was no wear on her uniform or equipment. Even her boots squeaked.

"Good. Spend extra time patrolling this neighborhood tonight, okay?"

"Yes, sir," she said.

She headed outside and walked past Palmer's car parked askew, partly on the sidewalk. I gave him a small grin. "Not wasting any time on your parking, I see."

"Not if I think someone's in danger."

There was a strength to his response that made me feel safe, like he would protect me no matter what. "I feel like I blew this out of proportion. I promise I'll lock the door when I get home, and I won't go out tonight." I didn't have any plans anyway, though he didn't need to know that.

"Do you live alone?" he asked.

"No. I live with my best friend, Abby.

There are five other apartments in the building. I'll be surrounded by other people and safe."

He frowned. "I'd rather see you at your family's house for the night."

My heart sank, because I knew if it came down to it, I'd let him take me there. I'd have to explain Frank's threat. Combine that with Trina's murder, and the aunts would fly into a protective furor. "How about I go to my apartment and I promise to call if anything seems wrong?"

He frowned. "You misunderstand what a cop means when he says he'd rather see something. It's a polite way to phrase an order. Grab your stuff, I'll take you to Proctor House now."

Really? An order? I took a deep breath to begin debating with him, then I thought of Abby, and Mrs. Thompson, and all the other people who lived in my building. Did they deserve to be put in danger, because I didn't want to talk to my family? That didn't seem right. At least my family was more than capable of protecting ourselves.

I let the sigh out. "Okay, you win. I'll go to the house."

It seemed like Palmer was forever driving me places in an attempt to keep me safe. I wasn't sure this was part of his job, but his protective presence comforted me. Despite not knowing him for long, I was beginning to trust him.

As we climbed into his car he said, "It's best if you keep to your normal activities for now. I'd like to give you some pointers about personal protection, in case anything happens when I'm not around."

"I'm not sure that's necessary. My cousins and I have taken about ten years of self-defense classes and, although I haven't been for a while, I still take Krav Maga lessons whenever I can."

He looked at me, eyes wide. He wasn't the first to be surprised at our ability to protect ourselves physically. He'd be even more surprised if he knew what we could do with a few self-defense spells as well.

"Krav Maga. I'm impressed. You don't strike me as a woman with a bloodthirsty, take-no-prisoners side. I suppose looks can be deceiving."

I laughed. "Having people underestimate me might be my greatest weapon."

"Where do you train?"

"We go to a gym in Greenland. They're super-nice, at least before and after the session. During the session, their goal is to push you as far as possible. It's intense. It helps to have Thea and Delia there with me, so we can all complain after."

"I'll have to check it out. Maybe we can spar together sometime."

I rolled my eyes. I wasn't sure he would be ready to spar with me, or any woman. He seemed more likely to protect than hit me. "Are you sure you're up to attacking a woman?"

When he braked at a stop sign, he turned to me. "Come at me or someone I care about with a weapon, and you'll see what I'm willing to do to protect others."

I knew I'd never take him up on that—at least not outside the gym.

When we got to the house, he parked and walked me in through the kitchen door. "This is getting to be a habit," I said. "At some point you're going to have to let me come home on my own."

"Once you're out of danger, you're free to come and go as you wish. For right now, though, it's important that you take extra precautions."

My mother threw a kitchen towel onto the table. "And exactly why is it you aren't safe now, Isabella?"

I turned to my mother. I hadn't noticed her in the corner of the room, and I regretted speaking freely. I shot a desperate glance at Palmer, hoping he would do something, anything, to get me out of this. Maybe I could ask him to arrest me? I was sure a night in jail would be better than explaining to my mother how I was in danger.

Palmer shrugged, as if to say it wasn't his job to navigate my family. He was right, but still—way to let a girl down.

"It seems the apothecary is in some

financial trouble that I'm going to have to work out. Frank, Trina's ex, thinks I should be giving him a thousand dollars a week. And, well, he sort of threatened me."

I sat down at the table, because saying that all aloud made my knees wobble. Sure, I knew how to defend myself both physically and magically, but I'd never had to before. I didn't look at my mother until I heard her choke off a sob. She sat next to me and pulled me into her arms.

"It's okay, sweetie. We'll work this out together as a family." Without letting go of me, she turned to Palmer. "Thank you for taking care of her. We'll make sure nothing happens from here."

Palmer cleared his throat. "We'll be keeping an eye on Frank, and if he tries anything, we'll be there." He paused for a moment. "This means we can't have any interference from the public, no matter how justified it may be. Don't go after him, don't seek him out, and don't communicate with him in any way."

My mother gave him a stony stare. She didn't take well to being told what to do.

Palmer was unfazed by her glare. "This means all of you. The whole family needs to stay out of his way, and don't think I won't arrest any of you for obstructing justice, because I will, for your own safety."

"Of course, Detective," my mother said in

her frostiest tone. "Thank you again."

With that dismissal, Palmer left.

"Your grandmother and I drove up to Sewall today and spoke with Hope. She had no idea what tea we were talking about," my mother said.

"Do you believe her?" I asked.

"I do. She allowed us to give her a truth potion, and she knew nothing about the poisoned tea."

"That's a relief, sort of. So who sent it?" I asked.

"I don't know. We tried to find traces of salvia before we left Sewall, but that was a dead end. We'll be much more careful of anything coming into the house from other people from now on."

I handed her Trina's letter, which she read in silence. She stood and I steeled myself for the inevitable storm she was about to unleash, but it never came. Instead, she called the rest of the family to the kitchen for a meeting.

Family meetings at our house have run the gamut from fun to serious to frightening. The only thing we could count on was raised voices and people disagreeing, even if the meeting was a fun one.

When Aunt Lily, Aunt Nadia, Grandma, Thea, and Delia had taken their seats at the table, my mother spoke. "Isabella is in trouble." She held up her hands to forestall any comments and continued, "It's not her fault. Trina had problems with her business that only came to light after her death. Unfortunately, they're falling to Isabella now."

"What's going on?" Grandma asked.

"Frank has threatened Isabella if she doesn't give him money every week." My mother paused for a moment to let that sink in.

"Does the business make that much?" Thea asked me.

"Possibly. Business might be different without Trina, though." I didn't have the strength to deal with this today, or maybe any day. I let my tears fall as my family kept talking around me.

"There's more," my mother said as she handed Trina's letter to Grandma.

Delia, who was sitting on the other side of me, put her arm around my shoulders. "Do you think we can talk about this later? Maybe let Isabella calm down a little?"

I lifted my head and looked at my family. Each was concerned for me, and I knew each would help. I felt protected here. Nothing would happen in this circle of strong women, and there was no mere man able to break our defenses. I took the tissue Delia handed me and composed myself.

"No, it's okay. The sooner we have a plan,

the safer we will be. Palmer wants me to continue life as normal, while remaining as safe as I can."

Grandma stood, clearly feeling better and energized when family needed help. "It's time for a self-defense refresher, then. We've been neglecting this area of training, because we didn't think we needed it. Now we do."

Thea rolled her eyes. "Krav Maga should keep me, Delia, and Isabella safe."

"It might, against someone with no magic. We don't know who might threaten you next," said Aunt Lily.

"What exactly did Frank say?" Aunt Nadia asked.

"He said Trina stopped paying him, and we saw what happened to her," I said.

The table went quiet for a moment. "He killed his ex-wife?" my mother asked, shock in her voice.

"Sure sounds like it. Palmer already suspects him," I said.

"Whether or not he killed her, he's threatening you, and we're going to need to put some rules in place," Grandma said. "These rules are nonnegotiable, because they are for the safety of the entire family. A threat to one of us is a threat to all of us, so we must all be as vigilant as possible. Is that clear?"

Grandma looked to each of us as we

nodded, the reality of the dangerous situation we were in hitting us. If we weren't all on guard, it would be easy for him to nab one of us to force the others to do whatever he wanted. "Our first rule has always been that we don't cast, hex, charm, or dose anyone without their permission. That's out the window for now. However, we're still responsible with our magic and we don't harm others with it. The cost to ourselves is too great. If you think you have to harm someone, think harder. There's always something else you can do."

I was amazed. For Grandma to dramatically change our first rule was stunning. Sure, the intent of not harming anyone was still there, although the actions we were allowed to take had opened up.

"We are all still responsible for keeping our powers a secret, as well. Imagine you're being chased by someone. What can you do?" Grandma asked.

"Tripping spell," Delia volunteered.

"Exactly. You can't make him trip out into traffic where someone else might hit him. We are still responsible for our actions and their consequences. Now, Delia, what is the tripping spell?"

Delia thought for a minute and said, "Clumsy feet, to you I speak, make this man tumble over and over."

"Good," said Grandma. "You can use confusion, invisibility, and shield spells, only if you have practiced them to perfection. That leaves you girls out."

"I'll cast protection spells on each of you later on tonight. That will help keep him away from us," said Aunt Lily.

My mother took my hand and said, "And until this is resolved, we don't go anywhere alone. I'd like you to stay here, as well. We can keep you more protected."

She didn't know I'd already had this conversation with Palmer, so her eyebrows raised when I said, "I think that's a good idea."

"Okay, now that this is settled, we still have a ceremony to get to," said Aunt Nadia. "You girls go get ready."

I'd forgotten all about the investiture ceremony tonight, and I wasn't feeling up to it. There was no way I was going to ask Grandma to postpone it. I'd be safer with Frank than if I did that.

Chapter 16

I picked up my robe from my bed. The berry-colored velvet I chose when I was fourteen was a bit bright for me now, but I still loved the color. My cousins had chosen darker colors, because they thought their older selves would prefer to be more sedate. At fourteen, I didn't care what my older self would like. I pulled the robe over my head, met my cousins in the hallway, and we silently walked to the back yard. These robes would be ours for our entire life, so they were cut like one-size-fits-all graduation gowns.

The aunts had set up our cauldron on the firepit we usually used for toasting marshmallows. Flame licked up around the edges, and I breathed in the warming scent of the fire. The small stone table we used for all ceremonies was set up in front of Grandma, with an athame on it.

The seven of us formed a circle around the cauldron—Grandma in orange, mom in brown, my aunts in navy, and then the three youngest witches in the family. Grandma and I were obviously the fashion radicals in the family.

Grandma cast an obfuscation spell along the border of our property to keep nosy neighbors away. "Hold hands," she commanded.

When the last two hands linked up, turquoise flame shot out from the wood under the cauldron. Next, we would declare ourselves after Grandma invoked the rites. We witches loved our poetry, although Grandma said she didn't have time to write all sorts of flowery words each time we needed to do something, so she called to the goddess in her own way.

Unorthodox? I supposed the woman in the orange robe was a bit unorthodox. I could only hope to be more like her every year.

"Goddess, join us and bless these women as they dedicate themselves to your arts," Grandma intoned.

I went first because I was older by three days. I picked up the athame on the stone table and turned to the cauldron. "I choose potions," I said, and cut off a small lock of my hair. I dropped the hair into the cauldron, and berry-colored steam rose up.

That was another good thing about choosing a bright robe. My steam was pretty. Delia and Thea's would be navy blue and brown. Boring!

I rejoined the circle and my mother gave my hand three quick squeezes—our code for "I love you." I squeezed back and watched as my cousins made their declarations.

Thea chose psychometry, and we struggled to see her dark brown steam. I'd never seen Thea have any sort of readings or feelings when in contact with objects. I guess she'd learn. Delia chose spellcasting, and the cauldron sent up no steam. This was bad. Delia had chosen wrong. Delia's spells were never good, which is why we made sure she practiced before we broke into the apothecary.

Seven years is a long time for one concentration, and it would feel even longer if you chose the wrong focus. My heart sank for Delia; she was in for a difficult seven years.

No one else came forward, because Grandma's investiture would be in July, her birth month, and the aunts' in October. Grandma closed the short ceremony with one more invocation to the goddess. "May your wisdom guide these women for the next seven years, and may we all use our powers for the good of all."

Leaf of Faith

I felt a rush through my bones and then tingling on my skin. I gasped and looked to my mother. "Let's go eat," she said casually.

We broke the circle and walked into the house.

The dining room was full of food Aunt Nadia had spent the day making. The sideboard had drinks and desserts, while the table had an enormous holiday-style meal laid out on it. Investiture day was a family holiday, and we loved to celebrate with food.

We sat and Grandma raised her wine glass in a toast. "To absent family, may their shades ever watch over us."

We replied with, "Absent family."

My mother raised her glass. "To the next cycle of learning—may we all grow stronger, kinder, and wiser."

"Hear, hear," we replied.

Aunt Lily stood. "I'd like to say a few words."

Of course she did. She always wanted to say "a few words" that would keep us from eating for at least another half hour. My stomach audibly growled—had I eaten an afternoon snack? I couldn't remember.

"Make it fast, Lily, the girls are hungry," Grandma said.

Aunt Lily frowned as she sat down.

Grandma rolled her eyes. "Now don't go getting into a huff, Lily. You can talk just as well while we're eating as not. No one is saying we don't want to hear what you have to say, but it's damn cruel to keep us waiting when that roast is begging to be carved."

Once we had filled our plates with roast beef, mashed potatoes, roasted brussels sprouts, gravy, bread and carrots, Aunt Lily started to speak. "I am proud of our young witches tonight. I know you will use your abilities to serve others."

Aunt Lily was very conservative in this way. She felt using our abilities for anything other than helping people was not right and a misuse of the gifts we were given. As a result, we were not as rich or famous as other families. On the other hand, we didn't have nearly the problems those families had, either.

I turned to my mother and said, "What was that I felt at the end?"

She brushed a crumb from her lip and said, "If you choose particularly well, you'll feel it "in your bones," as the saying goes. Is that what you felt?"

"I felt it in my bones and tingling on my skin. Is that good?"

She nodded. "It's good because your interests are aligning with your skills and your talent. You may find you never leave potions."

Interesting. I'd always thought I'd be the kind of witch who never settled down to just one thing—that I would keep choosing new topics of interest, just to shake things up.

I guess time would tell.

"I didn't feel that," said Delia.

Aunt Nadia squeezed Delia's hand. "We all have times when we don't choose as wisely as perhaps we could have. It's happened to me, to your aunts, and even to Grandma."

Delia looked down at the table. "First choice and I'm already doing it wrong. Can I go back out and choose something else?"

"It doesn't work that way," Aunt Nadia said. "You'll have to make do and learn as best as you can."

"You should expect your spells to go wrong often, but not always in the way you think," Grandma said.

We finished dinner in a more somber mood, and I thought I would try to find a way to help Delia cast better spells. Maybe if we practiced every day she wouldn't be too bad?

Rather than stay up late, we all went to our rooms to think about the terrible things besetting our family: Trina's murder, Frank's threats, Delia's investiture choice, and Grandma's poisoning.

Chapter 17

Trina's funeral was the following afternoon at Proctor House, in the lovely memorial garden. I locked the door to the shop, intending to walk until Detective Palmer parked in the empty spot in front of me.

"Can I give you a ride?" he asked.

I looked up at the sky. Dark, gloomy clouds obscured the sun, but at least the sleet was holding off for now. "I'm headed to my mother's."

"I thought so. I'm attending the service as well. Hop in."

I opened the door of his Toyota. Under his wool coat he wore a black suit, white dress shirt, and black-on-black tie. "Thanks. Did you know Trina well, or are you here to investigate the mourners?"

He gripped the wheel tightly. "She helped me with a case when I first got to town, and I always thought of her as a good person. I'm sorry she's gone."

I had no idea. Neither of them had mentioned this to me before. "She was one of the best. I don't how I'll get along without her."

He pulled out into traffic. "You'll be fine. You seem like a person who always lands on her feet."

I supposed that was true. Then again, at twenty-one, I hadn't had many challenges to speak of. I didn't have much else to say, so I stared out the window, watching people rushing to get home before the weather turned, until we got to the house.

I was amazed to see there were about thirty cars parked up and down our narrow street. We barely squeezed through to take the last available spot in the driveway.

"I'm going to make a quick call to the traffic division to see if we can get someone out here. It's going to be a mess when people want to leave."

I opened the door and got out of the car. "People won't all be leaving at once, not if my Aunt Nadia and her cooking have anything to say about it. Some people will be here past midnight."

He pulled out his cell phone. "Good to

know."

I left him to take care of business and mentally prepared myself to say goodbye to Trina. Once inside the house, I smelled Nadia's cooking in the kitchen and wanted to go in for a taste of the cheesecake. Grandma, dressed in a conservative black dress, stopped me at the front door.

"The aunts need your help in the back yard, getting people organized. We're starting in"—she glanced at the large grandfather clock in the front hall—"ten minutes."

I hustled outside to see at least a hundred people in our back yard. Most of them were witches, but there were several customers from the apothecary here as well. It was too early for the flowers in the memorial garden to bloom, but the green leaves of bushes and plants were out, promising a colorful spring. Thea was standing next to the stone table we'd used for our investiture ceremony, and a carved teak box rested on it. Next to the table was a folding chair.

"We need to get people to stand in circles around the table. Can you help?" Thea asked.

"Yes. Help me up onto the chair."

Once I was up, she held me steady while I waited for everyone to stop talking and look at me. "Thank you for your attention. The ceremony is about to begin, and the family asks for your cooperation. If you are related to Trina, please come forward and make a circle around the table now."

No one came forward. The Proctor women would be the only people in the smallest circle.

"And now, if you are a friend of Trina, please come forward and make another circle, holding hands, around the family circle," I continued.

Many people came forward and made a large circle.

"Finally, if everyone else would make one final circle, we will be ready to start."

I got down from the chair without falling, a minor miracle, and joined my cousins to create the family circle.

Detective Palmer escorted Grandma out from the house, flanked by my mother and aunts. He brought her to the inner circle and then joined the second circle, right behind me. He put his hand on my shoulder. "I'm here for you and your family, if you need me."

I smiled, even though he couldn't see me. I looked around the circles and saw so many people from the supernatural community that I'd lost touch with over the years. Abby and Bethany stood in the third circle, seeming unsure of what would happen next. Neither of them had seen a Proctor family funeral before, and they were in for a surprise.

Grandma cleared her throat, and the crowd slowly fell silent. "Thank you for joining us to say goodbye to our beloved relative, friend, and coworker, Katrina Bassett."

I turned my gaze back to the family circle and realized both Frank and Trina's nephew James were missing.

Had they not wanted to come? Even if they hadn't been on good terms before she died, surely they would want to come say goodbye and speak to her one last time.

Grandma opened the large, carved teak box that was resting on the stone table. "Proctor family custom is a little different than most funeral customs. Inside this box are small envelopes with Trina's ashes. We ask that you help us spread her ashes here in the memorial garden by coming forward and taking an envelope."

She held up an envelope to demonstrate. "We have plenty for everyone. Once you have your envelope, we invite you to find a spot in the garden and contemplate Trina for a quiet moment. It is our custom to say any last thing we want Trina to know, to send her on to the afterlife with the peace our love gives her, and then sprinkle her ashes. When we are done, we will meet in the house to continue by telling stories about Trina to each other so that she will live on in all our memories."

Leaf of Faith

The family circle moved forward and claimed their envelopes. I took mine to my favorite spot in the garden, the rosebush in the back corner, where I used to hide when I was little and my mother was angry with me. I thought the rose thorns would protect me from her anger, and I hoped they would protect Trina in the afterlife.

I opened the envelope. "Trina, I promise to work every day to be as good as you were to the customers and to the people in my life. I will miss you, but the things you taught me will be with me forever." I sprinkled her ashes at the base of the bush, watching as they floated down to the half-dead grass. I waited until they had all landed before I turned toward the house.

Detective Palmer was a respectful distance behind me, and as I walked to him, he offered me his arm. I linked my arm into his and we walked to the house.

"I've never seen this kind of funeral before," he said. "What religion does it come from?"

"It's a Proctor family tradition."

He nodded and didn't ask anything else.

We caught up to Chief Dobbins and Aunt Lily, walking similarly arm in arm. Aunt Lily was dabbing at her eyes with a lace handkerchief.

"I promise we'll find her killer, Lily," the chief reassured her.

She turned to him, anger in her eyes. "How are you going to do that, Ray?" she growled. "You have my niece as your prime suspect. My niece!"

Palmer cleared his throat. "Excuse me, Ms. Proctor, you have my assurance that Isabella is no longer a suspect."

Aunt Lily turned around and stared at us. She regained her composure. "At least your detectives are on the ball." She unwrapped her arm from the chief's and hurried into the house.

The chief seemed unworried and continued walking alone.

By the time we got into the house, it was filling up, and my cousins and I were pressed into duty bringing food to the various open rooms and making sure everyone had enough to eat and drink.

As people relaxed, it was nice to hear them laughing at the stories they were telling about Trina.

Palmer stepped up to be the bartender. I walked over to the makeshift bar in front of the living room fireplace. "I'd love a drink."

He eyed me warily. "Are you twenty-one?"

I gave him a playful punch on the shoulder. "You know exactly how old I am. It's in your paperwork."

"Will you be driving tonight?" he

continued to taunt me.

I raised my fist again, and he laughed. "I know, I know. No driver's license. What'll you have?" he asked.

I thought about it. I wasn't much of a drinker and only had experience with wine at dinners. "You choose, pick something you think I'll like."

He studied me for a moment. "I've got the perfect thing."

When he was done, he handed me a light orange–colored drink. "One breakfast martini for the lady."

I gave it a quick sniff and deduced the ingredients—gin, lemon juice, Cointreau, and orange marmalade. "Definitely not for breakfast."

Palmer smiled. "Not if you want to get anything done that day."

I took a sip. "Delicious. Thank you."

As I wandered through the thinning crowd in my house, I didn't see James or Frank.

I finished my drink quickly—that's the trouble with delicious drinks, you don't sip them. I turned the corner to the dining room and almost ran into a tall, gaunt man.

"Excuse me," he said, even though he had been the one standing still.

"No, no, excuse me," I said, manners still intact even though my nose felt a bit tingly.

He stared at me. "You're Isabella, right? The intern?"

I willed myself to focus. I had no idea I was such a lightweight. "Apprentice, and yes, I am Isabella." I held out my hand. "It's nice to meet you."

He took my hand and brought it to his lips. I pulled back a bit, because I didn't want his lips on any part of me.

"I'm Jake Forster. Glad to have found you. I was Trina's, ah, special friend, if you take my meaning. I've left some things at her house that I would like to get back with a minimum of fuss. You don't have the key to her house, do you?"

I shook my head. "No, I don't."

"She never had you go water the plants when she was away, collect her mail, anything like that?"

She never had. Then again, she hardly ever went anywhere. "Sorry, no."

"Well, no matter," he said as he put his hand on the wall next to me, keeping me from moving. "Perhaps you know someone who has a key?"

"You might check with—" I started before Palmer was suddenly next to us.

Palmer held out his hand. "Steve Palmer. How can I help?"

"Jake Forster. The young lady and I were

just having a conversation."

Palmer frowned. "Unfortunately, it's the young lady's turn to help me at the bar. Come along, Isabella."

I wasn't sure if I should slap him for treating me like I was eight or follow his lead to get away from this creepy guy. I looked at Jake and decided Palmer was by far the lesser of two evils.

When we got to the bar, Palmer said, "That guy is trouble, stay away from him."

Even though his words matched my intuition exactly, there was no way I would let his macho guy statement stand. "You thought I was a murderer. I'm not sure you're the best judge of character. Why should I trust what you have to say about Jake?"

"You're never going to let that go, are you? I've read his file. He's been arrested for bringing illegal exotic animals into the country, and when people get in his way, they tend to disappear."

I shuddered. Could he be Trina's killer? Had he approached her to sell some exotic ingredients, and then killed her when she refused and threatened to go to the police?

We watched as Jake stormed out of the house, and the mood of the room suddenly lightened. I'm not sure anyone else noticed it, but people started laughing again.

Chapter 18

The next morning, I was up and out of Proctor House before the rest of the family was awake. I needed time to think, and the best place for me to be alone was at the apothecary before it opened. I had to start making some progress on finding Trina's killer.

I sat at my table in the prep room and started making a simple tincture for coughs out of honey, ginger, and marshmallow root. Trina had been murdered six days ago, and the police didn't seem to have any suspects. I, on the other hand, had plenty. Frank, her ex-husband with the gambling problem may have killed her because she wouldn't give him enough money. Caroline Arneson might have killed her because she wanted to expand her tourist store into the apothecary's space. Her nephew James was angry at being fired and may have wanted to hasten his inheritance. Agatha, the customer who claimed Alice spoke to her, as kind as she was, was unbalanced enough that I couldn't rule her out yet. Jake Forster, the creepy man with the criminal record I met at Trina's funeral, could have killed her in a lovers' spat.

I had no evidence to rule any of them out yet.

I sat at my table and sketched out notes on each of my suspects until, at exactly nine o'clock, the phone rang.

I rushed to the office, picked up the phone, and in my best fake happy voice, I said, "Portsmouth Apothecary, how may I help you?"

"This is Arnold Lewis calling," said the raspy voice on the other end of the line.

"Good morning, Mr. Lewis. How may I help you today?"

"You know exactly how you can help me. I am sick and tired of calling you every few days to remind you that you still haven't made your December mortgage payment, and that you are in imminent danger of being foreclosed on."

Oh broomsticks! I needed to get a handle on the accounts. He thought I was Trina, and I wasn't sure if I should tell him she had died. Don't lawyers take care of that sort of thing?

"In fact, I'm quite surprised you bothered to answer the phone today. You haven't answered my call in at least a week."

"Mr. Lewis, let me stop you right here. I'm not Mrs. Bassett. I'm her apprentice. You shouldn't be discussing her finances with me." Maybe that would get me out of this conversation.

"Nice try, but I don't believe you, Mrs. Bassett. Here's what's going to happen. You're going to bring me the December mortgage payment by the end of business tomorrow, or I will have to garnish all your accounts with us until you're at least one month ahead with your mortgage."

That didn't sound right. I've never heard of anything like this, only evictions and foreclosures. "Wait a minute, you're going to take money from her other accounts? Can you do that?" I asked.

"Would I have suggested it otherwise?" he asked.

Yes, he might. "I thought the standard procedure was to evict or foreclose."

"I've been empowered to do whatever it takes for the bank to get the money you owe it. You have no standing here, at least not until you get current with your bills."

My eyes narrowed. I didn't like his tone, and I certainly didn't like being threatened. I paced the room. "As I've said, I am not Mrs.

Bassett. I'm her twenty-one-year-old apprentice. I don't appreciate the way you are speaking to me, and the fact that you don't even believe me. I'm sure you'll be in a lot of trouble when your boss finds out how you've handled this account and how you've been discussing your client's financial details with others."

He cleared his throat. "Really now, Mrs. Bassett, there's no need to make idle threats here. Particularly such weak threats. We both know you're not going to come down here and demand to speak to my manager, because that will get you immediately foreclosed on. You are, effectively, at my mercy, and if you don't do as I say, you'll find out what happens when I withdraw that mercy."

Of all the nerve! I would definitely be changing banks as soon as I was able — there was no way I'd work with this jerk. "I suppose time will tell, Mr. Lewis. In the meantime, I'd be careful if I were you. You don't want Trina upset with you — bad things happen when she is upset." I paused for a moment then continued, "You understand what I'm talking about, don't you?"

I could almost hear his gulp of fear. "It will soon be out of my hands. Get current on your payments now."

"Good day, Mr. Lewis," I said.

I hung up the phone without waiting to hear if he had anything else to say. I rubbed my sweaty palms on my jeans. Whatever ideas I'd had about how much fun it would be to run a business went right out the window, replaced by fears of not making enough money, not being able to pay the bills, and not being talented enough to help others on my own.

I needed help right away. I called The Fancy Tart, and Bethany was at my door in less than five minutes.

"All right, sweetie, let's get out all the books," Bethany said as soon as she came into the office. "I can't help you with anything until I read through all the transactions."

"I'm fairly sure I put them in the second drawer of the desk. You can look through all the drawers to find whatever you need."

"Do you mind?" she said as she gestured to Trina's chair.

It would be silly of me to worry about her sitting in Trina's chair, even though I wasn't ready for that step yet. "No problem. I'll be in the prep room, working on tomorrow's orders."

Before I went back into the prep room, I gave the sales floor a quick once-over. Everything was in its place, and the shop was immaculate.

After about thirty minutes, Bethany called me back into the office. "These books are . . . confusing at best."

"How so? Are they not set up like they

were when you first helped Trina?"

"You should probably sit down, this might take a while to explain," she said in a kind tone.

I sat in a visitor chair and leaned forward to look at the handwritten ledgers.

"The money coming in seems to be fine, but the money going out is a mess. It looks like she was taking cash out of the business without claiming it on taxes, and then funneling it to Frank. She began paying him two months after she opened, and the amounts have been getting progressively larger over time."

"How much?"

"Seven hundred fifty was the last payment she recorded in February."

I seethed. The nerve of him, asking me for even more than Trina was paying him just because he thought I wouldn't know any better.

"What about the regular bills? Have they been paid on time? And how about the mortgage?"

Bethany shook her head. "These are being paid sporadically at best. The problem comes down to the money she was giving Frank. If she hadn't given him anything, she would have had enough for all the bills and would have been able to pay herself a bit better as well. Assuming she leaves the business to you, I think you'll do just fine."

I relaxed in my chair, relieved. The business made enough money to survive. I just needed enough to replace my Fancy Tart salary and tips, so that I could devote myself to working one job.

I let a smile curve on my lips. "That's a relief, Bethany."

She walked around the desk and gave me a hug. "You'll let me know when or if you want to leave the Café, right?"

"Yes, of course."

"I'll hate to lose my favorite employee, but you'll have so many more opportunities here. You just need faith in yourself."

"I guess we'll know tomorrow whether I'll be leaving you or not. And speaking of favorite employee, Abby wants to impress you. She's disappointed because she thinks you don't notice all the extra hard work she puts in."

Bethany looked thoughtful. "Abby? I did notice she's started doing some things without needing to be reminded. I wondered what that was all about."

"If you don't mind, I'll spend more time training her how to work like I do, and then she'll be your favorite employee."

"We'll see how that works out," Bethany said.

Chapter 19

When I walked into the lobby of Trina's lawyer the next afternoon, I saw Frank, James, Detective Palmer, several apothecary customers, including Mrs. Thompson and Mrs. Canteford, and George Fiske, Caroline Arneson's lawyer.

Before I could stand next to Palmer, a trim, stylish paralegal announced, "Those of you here for the Bassett will reading, please follow me."

We all stood and walked down the carpeted hall to a conference room. The room had one large cherry table that seated eight and additional chairs lining one wall. A smaller table held a just-brewed pot of coffee, creamer and sugar, and several water bottles. The overhead lights buzzed, and I wished there was a window in the room so we could turn them off.

"Please make yourselves comfortable. There is coffee and water available. Mr. Shrewsbury will be with you in a few minutes," the paralegal announced.

I sat next to Ginger, a shy client who had hardly said more than two words to me over the past six months. She smiled at me, then dropped her gaze to her water bottle.

Detective Palmer stood by the door, even though there were a few empty seats around the table.

James sat next to me and leered. "Hoping to get something good? I'm sure I'm getting her business."

I was disgusted by his crass attitude. "I'm sure I'll be grateful for anything your aunt wanted to leave me."

James stretched and put his arm across the top of my chair. What were we? Back in middle school? He bumped his leg against mine and left it resting there. I tried to slide my chair away from the table to move to another seat, but he held it still.

Great. Now I was going to have to deal with this creep instead of paying attention to anything Trina had to say to me. I looked at Palmer, and apparently I telegraphed a call for help, because he covered the distance between us in a few steps and pulled James up by his collar.

"You sit there," he said as he pointed to a chair by the door.

I grinned at Palmer, hoping he'd sit next to me. Instead he stood by James, making sure he didn't move. It's good to have friends.

Mr. Shrewsbury came in and sat at the head of the table. He was a gaunt man with wispy white hair. He would have looked old except for his ramrod straight posture and brisk gait. "We are here to read the last will and testament of Ms. Trina Bassett. Anyone here not for that purpose should leave now." He surveyed the room for a moment. "Mr. Fiske, I don't believe you are needed here."

Fiske, Caroline's attorney, stood up, swiped his briefcase off the table and left.

After the door closed, Shrewsbury continued. "You will all receive a copy of the will when you leave, so I will get straight to the bequests. To my ex-husband, Frank Willis, I leave my house, which I will always consider 'our house.' Frank, I wish we were able to make it work between us because I have always loved you. There is one caveat, though, which is you may not sell the house for ten years. I want you to have a real home, someplace you can count on going to every night."

Frank scowled, not seeming to want the

house.

"To my nephew James, I leave my '95 Dodge Stealth. I've taken excellent care of it, and I hope that you will treat it as well as I have."

I couldn't see James, but I heard his whispered expletive. He expected to inherit the apothecary and instead got a car.

"To Isabella, my apprentice, my protégé, my friend. I leave you my business, Portsmouth Apothecary, with all its goods and funds to run as you see fit."

Did I hear him right? She left me the apothecary? She left it to me! My heart soared and I beamed, not caring that Frank was scowling at me. My mind raced with so many thoughts I couldn't pay attention to the rest of the bequests to Trina's friends and customers.

Not long after that, the reading was over. We stood and moved out to the lobby, where several people were milling around.

"Isabella, dear, I'd like to talk to you about my bequest," said Mrs. Canteford.

"Of course," I said, not remembering what Trina had left her.

"I've always admired the mirror Trina left me."

I nodded as I remembered. It was a lovely gilt mirror that gave the sales floor a sense of richness.

"Yes, well, I was wondering if tomorrow afternoon was convenient for me to pick it up."

"Absolutely, Mrs. Canteford. Whenever we're open, you can stop by." I didn't want to lose that mirror, because it fit perfectly between the front window and the herb shelves. I needed to find a replacement online tonight.

Mr. Fiske sidled up next to me. "Are you the new owner?"

"I am," I said, not able to keep the joy out of my voice.

Mrs. Thompson patted my hand. "You will do a lovely job, carrying on in Trina's footsteps. I know my Jameson's health is in good hands with you."

Her words warmed my heart. "What a lovely sentiment. I will do my best to live up to your faith in me. For now, I have to get back to work. I've got a lot of potions to make for tomorrow."

I had twelve orders today that I had not filled, and I promised each customer that the orders would be ready in the late afternoon. I had several more hours of compounding to finish before they were completed.

Before I left, James stormed past me, muttering, "Not even worth the effort. What a waste of time."

"Oh dear," Mrs. Thompson said.

"Someone hasn't been keeping up with his gratitude journal."

We giggled at that until we heard Frank shouting from the conference room. "What do you mean I can't sell it? How can that harpy dictate my life from beyond the grave?"

We grew somber and everyone else left. I took a seat in the corner of the room and continued to eavesdrop.

"The house is in a trust, and the trustee — that is me — is not allowed to let you sell for ten years," Mr. Shrewsbury said.

"That can't be legal," Frank said. "I'll fire you and get a new lawyer on it."

"You are certainly free to do that, though I'm afraid you'll be throwing money away. Why don't you accept this gracious gift she's given you and use the house as your home? I'm sure you'd be more comfortable than you are in your current location," Mr. Shrewsbury soothed.

I wondered where Frank lived. It had never occurred to me that he might not live somewhere nice. He drove a nice car and had well-tailored clothing, so I assumed he had a nice house, too.

"You know why I can't do that. If you're not willing to help, I'll find someone who will."

I watched as Frank stormed through the lobby and slammed the door as he left.

Mr. Shrewsbury closed the door to the conference room and I stood to follow him to his office. "Mr. Shrewsbury, could I have a minute of your time?"

He turned around. "Miss Proctor, is it? Certainly."

He led me to his office and invited me to sit. His office was surprisingly modern. His glass and chrome desk had only a closed laptop on it and behind the desk was a black Aeron chair. The black and gray carpet was surprisingly plush and matched the floor-to-ceiling drapes that I assumed hid a window.

He motioned to a black and chrome guest chair. "Have a seat. May I get you a drink?"

"No, thank you."

He pulled a folder from a filing cabinet. "Here is the bank documentation to sign in order to take over the accounts for the business. In addition, you should know Mrs. Bassett had a life insurance policy that will cover the mortgage on her storefront and take care of any outstanding bills she has."

What a relief! "Thank you. I'll need to rebuild our stock after the break-in."

Mr. Shrewsbury steepled his fingers. "I don't wish to be presumptuous, but do you have any experience running a business? I'm certain you can take care of the day-to-day operations and what you need to make for people. What I mean is can you file your taxes or payroll without making errors? Do you know how to read the contracts you must sign? Things of that nature."

My heart sank. In all my dreams of running a business, these legal and mundane things had never entered my mind. "I don't."

His eyes lit up. "My firm can handle these details for you, for our usual fee."

Before I could turn him down, he continued speaking. "You might think our fees are high," he said as he slid a sheet across his desk to me. "However, consider how much it will cost you if you get something wrong. Much better to be safe than to lose the business Trina gave you."

It was amazing. In the space of a few seconds, he'd gone from kind older man to sleazy sales pitch guy. My mind was screaming not to agree to anything, because he was going to take advantage of me and my ignorance.

"Thank you for your offer," I said as I took his list of fees. "I'll consider it and will call you once I've made my final decision." That should keep him off my back for a little bit. My first stop would be to talk to Bethany. She'd set up Trina's systems years ago and I was sure she could talk me through everything without costing me an arm and a leg.

He seemed surprised I didn't take him up

on his offer. "We are a very busy firm, Miss Proctor. It would be best if you retained us immediately."

Not going to happen. "Do you have time for a question?"

Shrewsbury looked at his watch. "I've got a few minutes before my next meeting."

"Is it true Frank can't sell the house for ten years? I mean, is that sort of stipulation legal?"

"Yes, it's legal. I wouldn't have allowed Mrs. Bassett to include it in her will if it wasn't."

"And where he lives now isn't as nice?"

Shrewsbury laughed. "He lives in a trailer park off Route One. Trina's house is a substantial improvement."

"Oh. I see."

I stood to leave and we shook hands.

"I hate to think what might happen to a young woman on her own with a business. Consider my offer carefully," he said.

As I left, I wondered if I was imagining it, or had he just threatened my business?

Outside, Detective Palmer was leaning against his car. "Can we talk?"

"I'm heading to the apothecary. I've got as much time as it takes you to drive me there."

"I suppose that will have to do for now. Hop in."

He started the engine. "You know these

people much better than I do. Did anything strike you as odd in that reading?"

I thought for a moment. "James has never hit on me like that. Thanks for coming to my rescue."

"Did the bequests seem out of line to you?"

"I am surprised she left me the business. I assumed she'd leave it to family and that maybe I'd be kept on to run it."

"Anything else? How about all the smaller bequests? It sounded like she was giving away half the shop right out from under you."

I sighed. "I wasn't listening to them very well. I was too excited by my inheritance. I'm sure I can replace anything she gave away. I think she was being kind to our most faithful customers— nothing insidious going on."

"Okay, I'll take your word on that."

"Frank wants to sell the house, though. He's got no interest in living in it."

"Really?" he asked.

"I heard him yelling, because he didn't bother to close the door while he demanded the lawyer fix it so he could sell the house."

"Interesting. Probably not motive for murder, though. The way to make money in real estate these days is to hold on to it and rent it out. You've got a steady cash flow for the rest of your life, if you do it right, and you'll make more than the house is worth in the end."

I thought about my own apartment. Abby and I each paid nine hundred dollars a month. There were six apartments and the building was old. Our landlord, Mr. Subramanian, was probably making a lot of money off us.

Palmer parked in front of the apothecary. "Have a good afternoon."

"Thanks. I'm going to figure out how to run a business."

"You know that takes people years to learn, right?" he asked.

I stepped out of his car. "I'll get a lot of on-the-job training."

Chapter 20

I opened our apartment door, disappointed that Abby had left the door unlocked. Again. Yes, we were in a safe building in a usually safe town. I didn't think we ought to tempt fate, though.

"Guess who's about to become Bethany's favorite employee?" I called out after I closed and locked our door.

Abby stuck her head out from her bedroom, a confused expression on her face. "Who?"

"You are! Trina left me the store in her will, and in a few weeks, I'm going to have to leave the bakery."

Abby ran to me and nearly knocked me over with her hug. "That's fantastic news! I'm so happy for you."

"I'm relieved. The more I worked there, the more I was certain that was my calling. At the same time, I didn't want to be Trina's competition. I thought I'd have to move."

"No!" said Abby.

I hung my coat up and poured myself a glass of water in the kitchen. "Can you imagine what my family would say about me leaving the town, or even the state?"

"I know! They'd never get over it. How was the rest of the will reading?"

"It was fine. Trina gave a lot of the decorations in the shop to our customers. I'll have to replace it all once I get the necessary paperwork to the bank. She gave her car to her nephew and her house to her ex. He didn't want the house to live in, and she specifically said he couldn't sell it for ten years."

"Who would put that kind of stipulation on a bequest? Maybe he has a habit of selling houses? My mom can figure that out for us," Abby said.

Abby's mom was a real estate agent and could look up house sales data. If there was any kind of pattern to his buying and selling, she'd find it.

"That would be great. Can you call her?" I asked.

I stayed up until eleven, reading websites

about how to successfully manage a small business and had an entire legal pad full of notes.

Three thirty came awfully early the next morning, and I struggled to get out of bed. If I didn't need to get paid for a few more weeks at The Fancy Tart, I probably would have rolled over and gone back to sleep.

No, that was a lie. I would have spent five minutes thinking about how great it would have been to fall asleep again, then I would have gotten up anyway, because there's no way I would leave Bethany stranded without enough people at the bakery.

I threw the blankets off and did my best impersonation of an enthusiastic person—smiling and moving with energy I didn't think I had. It was pathetic, but at least I was out of bed.

The aroma of coffee perked me up, and I thanked the goddess for small favors. I threw on jeans and a sweater, pulled my hair up and headed to the kitchen for what would be the first of many cups today.

Abby looked as awake as I felt, although she was already dressed and pouring coffee into travel mugs for us. "Ready to go in five?" she asked.

"Yeah." I reached for my star and unicorn travel mug. The first sip was heaven. The second took hold of my brain and started shaking things up.

"Thanks for this," I said.

We slipped on our shoes and headed out for work.

"I was thinking about Frank this morning," Abby said as we walked toward The Fancy Tart.

"You were? It's awfully early to be thinking about anything but coffee, isn't it?"

She gave me a wry grin. "I woke up at three. Before my alarm, so I got up. I'm acclimating to the new schedule."

I smiled. "What about Frank?"

"He'd only want to sell the house if he already owned one, right?"

I nodded and drank more coffee.

"Well, he owns a trailer. My mom emailed me after we went to sleep. He's owned several houses, and he sells them every two years or so."

"That's weird."

"Mom says it's something to do with taxes. They're less if you hold onto a house for two years or more."

I had no idea about that; my family had owned our house for centuries.

"With each sale, he turns around and buys a smaller, cheaper house and that leaves him with a lot of cash in hand."

Interesting. I don't understand; why

would he need cash in hand if he was getting money from Trina?

"Enough to live on?" I asked.

"Sure, if he was careful. I've seen his car, and it's very expensive."

"Does your mother have any idea where the money goes?"

"She didn't say. She just sent me the facts."

How much could he possibly owe?

I spent the rest of the walk wondering who killed Trina and why.

We clocked in just before our shift started. Bethany took one look at me and said, "You can work out back with me for now." She turned to Abby and said, "You get the dining area sorted out."

I put my apron on and joined Bethany in the kitchen.

Bethany scraped butter and sugar into the industrial mixer and turned it on low. "We need to talk."

"About what?" I asked.

"Frank is a gambler, and if you're not careful, he'll take you down with him. It's best to cut ties with him completely, right now, and let him find his own way in the world."

"But—"

"He's a grown man, Isabella, and he should be responsible for his own actions."

Leaf of Faith

She was right. His wanting to sell Trina's house made a lot more sense, as did his serial house selling and downsizing. He also now had a good motive for killing Trina. He needed money and assumed she would leave him more in her will.

I shuddered and wondered how to protect myself from him.

I pulled bread out from the cooler and arranged it on trays to take out to the front of the store. Bethany and I worked in silence until she interrupted my thoughts.

"Why don't you go out and help Abby with the customers," she said.

The clock read seven already. I'd been working on autopilot for hours now.

In the front of the store Abby was handling the line of customers admirably. I was impressed; all it took was a change in attitude and a little discipline to not stay up half the night, and she was fitting in well on the early morning shift.

Abby and I worked for three hours at the counter until Bethany came out from the kitchen with a small cake. She'd frosted it and written "best wishes" on it for me.

I tried not to tear up. This had been my first job, and I'd been here for five years. "I'm not leaving yet, though."

"You will be soon enough."

I should have made some sort of speech, but I didn't know what to say, so I hugged her instead, took my cake and walked the two blocks to my apothecary.

I went in through the back door and took a moment to survey the office. It was exactly how I left it, and I'd have to get used to it being mine. I walked across the sales floor to unlock the front door, surprised to see a couple people waiting outside. They must really need their orders.

"Come on in and give me a second to get organized," I told them.

At the register, I lit the candle and touched Trina's photo. "Looks like it's you and me today," I said and got to work.

Once the shop had cleared out, Trina's nephew James came in.

"Good morning, James. How are you today?" I asked.

"I'm doing okay, considering. I was wondering if we could talk," he said.

I wasn't a big fan of his, and there wasn't much he was going to say to me that I wanted to hear. On the other hand, maybe he wanted to talk about Trina.

"Sure. What's on your mind?"

The door chimes rang and the letter carrier walked in. I felt relieved to not be alone in the store with James.

Leaf of Faith

"You're busy, so why don't I swing by here at six. We can go get a drink and relax a little."

The only thing I wanted to get after work was a good night's sleep.

"I can't today. How about tomorrow?"

"Great, it's a date. I'll meet you here."

I couldn't let that stand. "It's *not* a date, James. We're just two people who lost someone special to them, reminiscing over a drink." I hoped that's all we would be doing.

"Whatever," he said as he opened the door. "Six o'clock tomorrow."

The door closed and my heart sank.

Chapter 21

At the end of the day, I stood in the office doorway, looking at the desk. My desk. With hesitant steps, I walked around it and gently lowered myself onto the leather office chair. I needed a short break before I finished working for the night.

"I hope I don't let you down," I whispered, hoping somewhere Trina heard me.

Ten minutes into my break, the door chimes rang. It was probably just as well; I had work to finish.

I walked out of the office expecting to see a customer, but instead, Frank stood there. I gasped when I took in his face. Both his eyes were black and his nose was swollen. "Are you okay?" I asked.

He walked around, inspecting the mostly bare shelves. He winced as he moved closer to me, then stopped. "Don't worry about me. I overdid it at the gym."

I looked Frank up and down. There was no way he'd seen the inside of a gym in years. He had an unhealthy paleness to his complexion and was definitely carrying a few too many pounds.

"You know why I'm here, and what I need. I hope you're not going to be a problem," he threatened.

I took two steps toward him and stopped as he stumbled backward. "What is it about you? I've been trying to come in here all day for the money you owe me. Every time I get close to the door, I hurt all over."

Aunt Lily's protection spell for the win! He must have been really desperate to endure the pain. The poor guy. He didn't want to be here. Something, or someone, was forcing him.

"Are you sure I can't get you something? I've got a few potions that—"

"No potions," he spat. "I never used them, not even when Trina and I were married."

I thought for a moment about what I had in stock. "At least let me give you some arnica for the bruising. It's not a potion, it's a homeopathic remedy that lots of people swear by."

He waved his hand as though to push me

further away and took another step back. He stood up straighter, apparently having moved past the range of the spell.

"Money is what I need. You don't have to pretend to care about me or that I'm in pain."

"But I do care. Working with Trina this past year has shown me that it's my place in the universe to care for and heal others. It's no bother, honestly. What kind of person would I be if I let you leave here in pain when I can help?"

One side of his mouth lifted in a half-smile and suddenly I was looking at the Frank I remembered from a year ago. Friendly, kind, always ready with a bad joke. He took a step toward me and all traces of the old Frank vanished.

"You inherited the store, you inherited the debts. One thousand a week."

"Trina had life insurance. I'm sure you could put in a claim with Shrewsbury and get the debt paid off."

He frowned. "You don't understand how this works. It wasn't an official loan, with papers drawn up. She used our money and would be paying it back for a very long time."

He took another step forward and grunted. "Money, now."

I didn't have a thousand dollars to give him, and that was a good thing, because I felt like

I'd do anything to get him to leave. "I'm sorry, I can't."

He took one more step forward and almost fell to the ground. "They'll kill me if you don't. If you care about me as much as you say you do, you'll save my life and give me the money."

His face writhed in pain as he tried to take the last step to get to me. His agony was my fault, and I hurt just seeing him wince.

I cast a confusion spell on him. "Mist of the mind's eye, remove these thoughts and let him go forth with calmness."

I watched to see if the spell worked. Grandma told us not to use it unless we were sure it would work, but I couldn't think of anything else to get him out of the shop.

He took two steps back and straightened up. His eyes refocused as he took in his surroundings. I knew he'd be in a susceptible, almost hypnotic, state for the next few minutes.

"If that's all, Mr. Willis, I hope your move to Antigua is as lovely as you say it will be."

"Antigua?" he asked.

"Yes. I believe you're packing up and taking a flight tonight. You want to start over and live a simple life, happy with whatever money you have."

"That seems . . . like a good idea," he said. "Have a good evening."

Frank left the store walking with a lightness he'd never had before. I truly hoped he moved to Antigua and had a happy new life.

With shaky hands, I locked the door behind him and turned the sign to "closed." I poured myself the last of the lemon chamomile tea in a china cup. I'd drink the tea, calm my nerves, and then go home.

As I sat in the office, wondering about Frank, I realized Thea and Delia could watch him to make sure he got on the plane. I picked up my phone and dialed their office. "Hi, it's me. Don't worry, but Frank was just here."

"Are you okay?" Thea asked.

"Yeah, I'm fine. I cast a confusion spell on him and told him he was moving to Antigua."

"And he didn't hurt you?"

"No, honestly, I'm fine. I need your help though."

"Name it and we're on it," she said.

"He lives in the trailer park off Route One. Follow him until he goes through airport security. Stay far away, though, because the protection spell worked well, and he was in a lot of pain when he was close to me."

"You got it. We'll leave now and I'll keep you updated."

"You're the best," I said.

"You owe us big now. You might never get

out of debt to us."

I laughed as I hung up. My cousins owed me as many favors as I owed them.

I finished my tea and considered calling Palmer, but decided not to. There was no way I could tell him the truth—the spell worked, and I made Frank decide to move far away. He'd never believe me, and he'd never take me seriously again. Even worse, if he did believe me, he'd be afraid of me and my abilities. It happened to the aunts and it might happen to me just as easily. Best to keep my secrets to myself.

I stood up and scanned the shop. I washed the teapot and my cup. I grabbed my coat and headed for my apartment. I'd call the aunts from there to let them know we were all safe as soon as I knew Frank was on his plane.

Chapter 22

The next afternoon, I started to get nervous. I'd been able to put the meeting with James out of my mind for most of the day because I'd been busy with customers or people coming in to talk about Trina.

At five of six, he was there, waiting for me as I finished closing up. He wore jeans with a hole in the knee, a tan hoodie with a grease stain down the front, and Timberland boots. He stood by the door and tapped his foot impatiently. What a jerk. I was tempted to tell him something came up, and I couldn't make it tonight.

I stretched closing as long as I could, but by ten past six, he said, "Aren't you done yet? Can't all this wait for the morning?"

I scowled at him. "I'm ready to go. Where

to?"

"We're going to The Lips. I've got a friend working there tonight and so we'll get cheaper drinks."

Great. The name of the bar was actually Loose Lips Sink Ships Tavern, and it was the worst bar in town. Cheap drinks in a cheaper bar. I was hoping he'd pick somewhere I could walk to, but it was five miles away, so I opened the door to the Dodge Stealth Trina left him and got in.

He slid into his seat and pulled the car into traffic. "Have the police told you anything about the investigation? I saw you talking to that detective outside your apartment building."

"You did?" That was creepy. Had he been stalking me for the last few days?

"Yeah. Do you know Chuck, he lives in your building? He's my best friend and I was at his place."

That made more sense. But to admit to having Chuck as a best friend? This didn't make me think any more highly of him.

"Oh, I didn't know that. I've never seen you around before." I looked down at his feet. "Can I ask you about your boots?"

He looked at me, brows furrowed. "Yeah, I guess. They're just boots."

"Timberland, right? Are they really waterproof? I don't have a car and need better boots for walking in the winter."

"You don't have a car? Who doesn't have a car?"

"What size are yours?" I winced at the directness of my question.

He laughed. "What size are my shoes? Is that really the question you want to ask?"

"Just curious. I wear a nine."

"Mine are twelves. And yes, they're waterproof."

Size twelve. Two sizes larger than the print found in the apothecary's office. I relaxed my shoulders, relieved James wasn't a murderer.

It had been a long time since I'd been in this part of town. Several shops were empty and covered with graffiti, their parking lots not even plowed. Not having a car meant I usually spent my time within walking distance of my apartment. I didn't need to go much further than that most times, so it didn't bother me to walk everywhere.

When we pulled up to the bar, I frowned. It was seedier than I remembered: Peeling white paint appeared grey in the waning sunlight, a broken window was taped over with duct tape, and the glass door was covered with metal security bars.

"Charming," I said.

"Yeah, well, it's not some fancy downtown

place, but my buddy won't rob us blind on the drinks, and I don't need to watch my manners."

Great. How to get myself out of this as fast as possible? I should have set up an "emergency" call with Thea and Delia. Instead, I was out here on my own.

I considered waiting until he opened the car door for me, but thought that was a wasted gesture—he wouldn't even realize what I was doing. So I walked in and stood at the bar as close to the door as I could.

I needed to because there was almost no light in the room, and there was no way I was going to sit in a dark corner with him where no one could see us. The scent of stale cigarettes and day-old spilled beer assaulted my nostrils. I forced myself not to examine the smells any further—I was afraid what I might learn. There were no other customers in the bar and my heart sank. I really didn't want to be alone with James.

The bartender turned to us and looked me up and down appraisingly. "Shit, man. You weren't kidding," he said to James.

Some people have sleeve tattoos—the bartender had a turtleneck of tattoos, and it looked as though once he had enough money, they were going to cover his entire face.

"Hands off, she's mine," James said as he put his arm around me.

Not again. I didn't need a repeat of his middle school crush behavior from yesterday. Rather than shrug him off me, I took a step back and ground my heel into his foot. He flinched and took his arm away from my waist.

I sat on a stool and glowered at James.

"Let's get a table," he said.

"I'm fine here." I smiled at the bartender. "Corona in a bottle." I've never liked beer, but I really didn't want Tattoo Neck making me a drink.

The bartender opened a bottle for me. "Would the lady like a lime?"

The cutting board out on the counter had a dark streak across it, and I decided I didn't dare risk food poisoning.

James ordered a shot of Barton vodka. I winced for him. That was going to go down like diesel fuel. But I supposed if you feel like you've got to get wasted, this was one of the fastest and most economical ways to do it.

I sipped my beer, determined to make it last. When James didn't say anything, I said, "So, what's going on?"

"Drink more first, then we'll talk," he said.

Tattoo Neck brought him another shot and I took a sip of my beer. It was bitter—more bitter than I remembered beer being. After his third shot and my third sip, the beer wasn't tasting so bad anymore, and I was feeling much more relaxed.

The bartender nodded at James, who pulled a sheaf of papers from his jacket pocket and put them in front of me.

"Isabella," James said.

It seemed to take more energy than usual to move my head. I giggled at the idea that anything required energy as I swung my head back and forth. A wave of dizziness hit me, and I grabbed onto the bar so I wouldn't fly off my seat.

"Woah! I don't feel so good," I said. The bar was sticky, and I laughed at how it tried to hold my hand down.

"Isabella, focus," James said. "I need you to do me a huge favor and sign these for me."

He took my hand away from the sticky section and put a pen in it. The pen wasn't nearly as much fun, so I dropped it and went back to testing the sticky bar.

James vanished from my sight, then reappeared holding the pen. I clapped at his trick. "You disappeared!" I said in awe.

"Jesus, Mick, how much did you give her?" James asked.

The bartender shrugged. "How did I know she was such a damn lightweight?"

The pen reappeared in my hand. I had no idea James could do tricks like that. No, wait. These weren't tricks. He was magic, like me.

"You're magic and you never told me!" I

accused before I burst out laughing.

"Focus, Isabella, sign the papers," James barked.

He was so serious. I pulled away from him, afraid of what he might do.

"I'll be out back if you need me," the bartender said.

"Sign the papers, and I won't yell at you again," he said, trying to coax my hand near the papers.

That sounded like a good idea. If I signed, we could get back to our night out. I could try to turn my head faster and faster until it spun right around. Fun!

I looked from my hand to the paper. My arm felt heavy as I moved it to the page. I missed, and knocked his empty shot glass over onto the floor. It cracked and reflected the fading light from the door. "Oh, pretty!" I said.

James snapped his fingers in front of my face. "Hey, pay attention."

I squinted at his face and tried to remember what he wanted me to do.

"Sign the papers," he said.

I moved my arm again, and this time the pen was on the paper. I signed in my prettiest handwriting—the signature I made when I was in eighth grade, with a heart for the "a" at the end of "Isabella." I lifted the pen up and dragged my head over to peer at him. "Not there, you idiot."

He picked up my hand and put it so the pen was on the signature line. "Oh, you want me to sign here," I said. I started to sign when I heard my cousin Delia say, "Isabella? Stop!"

All this moving my head around was exhausting, so I set it down on the bar. I hit the sticky spot and rolled my forehead back and forth on it, giggling. I didn't understand why I heard Delia's voice until I was being picked up from the stool. Delia and Thea were peering at me.

"Hey! When did you get here?" I asked.

Thea swiped the papers off the bar before James could get them. I guess four shots slowed him down. I shouldn't talk, though, three sips and I was wasted!

"Let's go," Delia said.

They dragged me out of the bar and put me in the back seat of Aunt Nadia's SUV. Delia squealed the tires as we left the parking lot. "Where are we going?" I asked, but I never heard their answer.

I woke up to something jabbing me in the arm. I opened my eyes, but screwed them shut again because the light hurt. "Ow!" I yelled. I tried to swat at the pain, but my other arm didn't move very well, and I wound up smacking myself in the face.

"Isabella?" I heard my mother's frightened

voice.

"Yeah, I'm here," I said, but where was I?

I opened my eyes again and saw her standing over me. Behind her was a woman in scrubs.

"Why am I in the hospital?" I asked.

I shook my head and things started to become clearer.

"The treatment is starting to take hold. She'll be more coherent in a few minutes," the nurse said.

My mother raised the head of my bed. My whole family was around me, and behind them I could see Detective Palmer.

My mother kissed my forehead. "Thank the goddess you're going to be okay."

Palmer moved in front of Thea. Wow, was he handsome. I thought I should tell him that, but a small part of my mind knew I'd be embarrassed if I did, so I squeezed my lips shut.

"Is she ready to answer questions?" he asked the nurse.

"You can try, but if the answers don't make sense, you'll have to try again later."

"I'm going to have to ask everyone to leave," Palmer said.

Grandma scowled, but Aunt Lily took her by the arm. "She'll be safe with him, and we'll be right outside if she needs us."

I pressed the button to raise my bed higher so I was sitting up straight. I was grateful to see I was in my clothes and not a hospital gown. There was an IV running to my arm and the bag read "saline," so I thought I was probably okay.

"Why am I here?" I asked before he could say anything.

"You were roofied," he said.

An icy dread crawled up my spine. "What? How?"

"Well, maybe it was because you went to a dive bar with a strange man?" He ran his fingers through his hair. "What were you expecting?"

Anger roiled in my stomach. "Excuse me? I went to a bar in the town you are supposed to protect, with a man I knew. I did nothing wrong here, and it seems to me that you let me down, Buster."

"Buster?" he said.

"Yeah, Buster. If Thea and Delia hadn't come in, I don't even know what would have happened."

He let out a long sigh. "It wouldn't have been good, that's for sure."

I tried to think back to my time at the bar, but it was all hazy. "I don't remember much after we walked in and the guy with tattoos handed me a beer."

"Do you remember James trying to get you

to sign some papers?"

I closed my eyes and saw myself writing the heart at the end of my signature. "I do, I think. I thought he wanted to see my name, so I used my signature from eighth grade." I winced as I remembered. It was so girly and cute. "I'd replaced the last "a" with a heart. Oh, goddess. How embarrassing!"

He grinned and held up an evidence bag with my scrawled name across the top. "It's adorable, what are you talking about?"

"Oh, stop it," I said. "There's no need to embarrass me like that. I'm horrified enough as it is."

Palmer pulled up a chair and sat next to my bed. "The paperwork is to get you to sell the shop to him for a dollar. We've got warrants out for James and the bartender, who ran before we could get to them."

That rotten, no-good . . . jerk! When he didn't get what he wanted from Trina, he tried to steal it from me.

"I don't understand how I got roofied. I ordered a bottle of beer, he opened it in front of me, and I didn't leave it alone for a second. How could anyone slip something into my drink?"

"If the bartender was in on it, he could have slipped the drugs into the bottle before he gave it to you."

Damn. There wasn't any way to stay safe if someone was determined to take advantage of me. On the other hand, a lot of people had tried lately, and I'd managed to avoid doing what they wanted. Frank was gone to Antigua, Caroline had promised me she would leave me alone, and I'd deftly deflected two different lawyers. Maybe I wasn't doing so bad after all.

"Was there anything I could have done?"

"Not really. I guess you could have had nothing to drink at all. Or you could not go out with guys who want to hurt you."

"It wasn't a date. I thought we were going to talk about Trina, you know, commiserate on our loss. I've never liked him and didn't really trust him, but I didn't think he'd stoop so low."

He patted my hand. "I know. The hospital is going to release you, and I want you to go to your mother's house tonight."

I rolled my eyes. "I'll never hear the end of it if I do," I said.

"That might be true, but you'll be safe and I won't have to worry about you while I hunt down this lowlife."

The effects of the drug were almost gone, but as I gazed into his brown eyes, I resolved not to tell him how I would feel safe knowing he was protecting me. And I definitely wasn't going to tell him how handsome he was. Nope. Not me. I was going to play it cool and let him make the first move.

"You would worry about me?" I asked.

He nodded. "Your apartment building doesn't have particularly great security. Anyone could get into those apartments if they wanted to. Being on the second floor doesn't help, because it's too easy to climb onto the roof of the porch and slide one of your windows open."

Had he specifically thought about my safety, or was it an occupational hazard that he assessed the safety of every building he saw?

"It's nice to know you care," I said.

He took his hand from mine. "It's my job." He stood up and said I could call him at any time if I remembered anything else from James or the bar.

"I will," I promised. And this time I meant it.

Chapter 23

My family took me to Proctor House and sent me straight to bed. I dozed off for a while, then woke up to light tapping.

"It's just us," Delia whispered. She walked in and flipped on the light.

Thea put a towel across the floor in front of the closed door to block the light. There was no sense letting the aunts see I was up at two in the morning.

My cousins, the most wonderful people in the world, had brought me food. I didn't realize I was hungry until I saw the sandwich and chips on the plate Delia was holding.

I sat up. "You two are amazing."

Thea handed me a can of ginger ale and a small glass vial. "The aunts have finally gone to sleep. You should have heard them arguing about you!"

I could only imagine. Hopefully, they got it all out of their systems and would be more reasonable in the morning.

"Grandma says you need to drink the potion, or else you're going to have a vicious hangover."

The potion contained licorice root, honey, and rose hips. I drank it down and followed it with a chip to get the taste of licorice out of my mouth.

Thea took the empty vial and slid it into her pocket. "We can go if you want to eat and go back to sleep, or we can stay with you for a while if you want."

Delia looked at me with tears in her eyes. I took the plate and set it on the bed. "Come here, you two," I said, and I grabbed them both in a hug. "If it hadn't been for you, things might have turned out very differently. You're my heroes."

Thea sat on the bed. "Thank you. I'm glad someone recognizes that. The aunts were all over you about being safe, but didn't take a single second to talk about how we were there and dragged you to safety."

I took a bite of the ham and cheese sandwich. The salty ham made my mouth water and my stomach gurgled in appreciation. "How did you find me?"

Delia took a potato chip from my plate. "We saw you leaving with James and followed you. You didn't know him in high school like I did. He was always the guy you didn't want to be left alone with."

Good to know my creepy-guy radar was working. "You followed me on a hunch?"

They nodded and I burst into tears. I hadn't realized how close to real danger I was tonight. What would he have done to me once I signed the paperwork? He wouldn't have driven me home and left me alone, most likely. If he was the kind of guy women didn't want to be alone with, well . . . I didn't even want to think about that.

My cousins hugged me tightly and whispered reassuring words to me. I didn't have the heart to tell them I wasn't sure if I'd ever feel safe again.

"We didn't get the chance to tell you yet—we followed Frank to Logan Airport. He took a non-stop flight to Antigua," Thea said.

"But the funny thing is, he stopped at a house first and dropped off his car and a gym bag before he took a cab," Delia said.

"A cab all the way to Boston?" I asked.

"It looked like Frank was paying someone off. The guy wasn't happy at first. He took money out of the bag and shook it at Frank. That's when

Frank handed over his keys and watch. The guy looked a little happier and went inside. I thought we were going to get caught, sitting on the side of the road like that, waiting for Frank to leave," Thea said.

We talked for a while longer about funny things, childhood memories—anything to keep my mind from worrying until I started to fall asleep. They tucked me in and promised one of them would stay with me all night.

True to their word, Thea was asleep on an air mattress next to my bed when I woke up in the morning. I slipped out of the bed, trying not to wake her, and padded downstairs to the kitchen.

I needed coffee, because even though I drank Grandma's potion, I still didn't feel great. I opened the kitchen door and to my horror, Palmer was at the table with Grandma, eating breakfast.

I'd borrowed pajamas from Thea and felt too exposed in the tank top and boxer shorts I had on. I ran upstairs to put on my clothes from yesterday, but I couldn't find them on the chair where I had left them.

Instead, a fresh set of clothes was sitting at

the foot of my bed, and Thea had woken up. "Whose clothes are these?" I asked Thea.

"They're mine. I picked what I thought you'd like best."

Had I mentioned how awesome my cousins were?

"Detective Palmer is having coffee down in the kitchen with Grandma. Make sure you get dressed before breakfast," I warned.

Her eyes went wide. "He saw you in the jammies?"

I blushed. "Yeah. Now get out so I can get dressed and see why he's here."

When I got downstairs, the aunts had joined Grandma and Palmer in the kitchen. No one mentioned my ungraceful exit earlier. It must be bad, if the aunts were holding themselves back from teasing me. That wasn't the way we did things in my family.

I poured myself a cup of coffee and sat at the table. "Detective, good morning. What brings you here?"

"Your family threatened me in all sorts of unpleasant ways if I didn't keep them, and you, updated on the hunt for James."

I took a large sip, letting the strong taste wake me up. "So, Buster, where is he?"

Palmer grinned. "I didn't think you'd remember calling me that yesterday. You seemed out of it."

"By the time we were talking, I was fine."

He furrowed his brow. "You never stopped talking."

Bats! I thought I had passed out. If I never stopped talking, did I say anything embarrassing? I was afraid to ask.

"Okay then. I guess I don't remember it all. Where's James?" I asked.

"We're not sure. We tracked his car to the train station in Dover, and he bought a ticket to Boston. After that, we don't know where he went." Palmer replied.

To steady my hands, I wrapped them around my coffee mug. If he was still out there, did he want to hurt me again?

"What do you mean, you don't know?" my mother said.

Aunt Lily picked up the house phone. "That's ridiculous. I'm calling Ray right now."

Palmer raised his hands to calm the room. "We don't think Isabella is in much danger. He failed in his attempt to get her to sign, and if anything comes up with her signature on it, of course we're going to be suspicious. We think he'll lay low for a while, possibly leave the area permanently."

"And if he tries again?" Aunt Nadia asked.

"We'll be ready."

"We?" I asked.

"I'm having Kate stay with you for the day."

How unsafe did he think I was going to be, in broad daylight, with customers coming in and out? "I doubt that's necessary."

"Do as he says," my grandmother said.

Great. If I disagreed, I'd be browbeaten into agreeing anyway. Sometimes I wondered why they never understood why I moved out.

"It's okay. I'll feel safer with her there," I said.

"I'm spending a good portion of the day talking to other businesses in the area, and I'll be no more than a few blocks away," Palmer said.

That made me feel better. If Palmer was going to be close, I'd feel safe at work.

I glanced at the clock. It was only seven thirty, and I wouldn't open until ten.

"I'll be back in an hour to drive you," he said. "I don't want you walking or leaving the shop today. If you need to go somewhere, I want to be the one to take you. Just in case."

My day was starting to look up. I had a handsome police officer who seemed to want to stay close to me, at least as a bodyguard.

"Thank you. I appreciate your concern."

He stood up, thanked Grandma for the coffee and left.

Once the door closed, I turned to Grandma. "You are suspiciously quiet this morning."

"I didn't need to do anything; it was all going according to plan."

"What plan?" I asked.

She didn't answer. I was used to her not answering questions she didn't want to. Grandma had plans that could take years to develop, and I'd learned it was almost always useless to try to get her to say anything she didn't want to, so I gave up, went upstairs and got ready for the day.

By the time I came downstairs, Palmer was in the kitchen, chatting with my mother. Nothing good would come from this, that was for sure.

"Ready to go?" he asked.

I grabbed a muffin from the table. "You bet."

I was surprised when he didn't hold the door open for me to go through first. When he stopped to survey the gardens before we left the kitchen, I realized he was serious about keeping me safe. On the one hand, this was good. On the other, worrying. If I might not be safe walking in my driveway, things might not be as safe as he was letting my family believe.

I followed him outside once he moved.

"A cruiser?" I asked. "I'm going to look like I've been arrested."

Leaf of Faith

He opened the passenger door for me. "Only if you sit in the back seat. The front seat is for non-criminals only."

I was only teasing. Apparently, he wasn't in the mood. For the short drive he never stopped scanning the street, making sure he knew what was happening all around us.

He parked by the now-empty greenhouse. I was going to have to order new plants this week.

Kate stepped away from the building, and he rolled down his window. "Hey, Detective. Nothing to report this morning."

He held his hand out to me. "Keys?"

I handed him the keys, which he then handed to Kate. "Once she finishes checking the premises, we'll go in."

"When you say Kate's going to stay with me all day, what exactly do you mean?" I asked.

"She'll keep an eye on you and everyone who comes in. She won't be in your way."

"She's not going to interrogate my clients, is she?"

He laughed. "No. She'll watch what's happening on the sales floor, do occasional outside checks, things like that."

I didn't know how to feel about this. Sure, I felt safe with my own personal officer, but wasn't this a waste of resources? I couldn't imagine that many people got this option.

"Doesn't she have more important things to do?" I asked.

"Please, Isabella. Don't argue with me," he said.

"Excuse me?" I replied with more heat in my voice than I should have used with someone who was trying to keep me safe.

"Listen, I won't be able to focus on finding James if I think you're not safe. With her here, I can do my job better and faster."

I scowled. "You should have asked me first."

"And you would have said no. At least according to your mother."

That's what they were talking about in the kitchen. I definitely didn't like the idea of the two of them ganging up on me like this.

"Fine. Today only."

He nodded. I didn't believe for one second that he was actually agreeing with me though.

Kate came to the car. "All clear, boss."

She led me into the shop and handed me the keys. I lit the candle next to Trina's photo with a match, in case Kate was watching. "Good morning, Trina."

Kate looked at me a bit funny. "You're talking to a picture?"

"I miss her, you know? Saying good morning to Trina makes walking into the shop feel less lonely."

Kate nodded. "I can see that. Anyway, I'd like to talk for a couple minutes about how the day is going to go."

I unlocked the office. "Let's have a seat in here."

I was pleased with her plan. She wanted to sit in the prep room, out of the way, and peek out once in a while to keep an eye on the customers. It was my job to tell her if anything was wrong. She'd do a perimeter check every hour, too.

The morning flew by, and at noon, Aunt Lily stopped by with two lunch bags for Kate and me. She placed them on the counter. "How's your day going?"

"Very dull. Just waiting on customers and tidying up." I picked up one bag to bring to Kate, who was sitting in the prep room. "Thanks for the food."

"Your mother insisted I bring it to you. She wanted a family member to check in on you."

"Why didn't she come herself?"

"Your grandmother has decided to move her entire library from the first floor to the third floor, and she's making your mother do all the work."

I rolled my eyes. My poor mother.

"And if you still need watching tomorrow, all the books will get moved back to the first floor," Aunt Lily continued.

"Mom will never put up with that," I said.

"Of course she will. We all know why Grandma's doing this, and your mother is going along with it, because it's the only thing keeping her from worry. She'll be so exhausted tonight that she'll actually sleep, too."

"She didn't sleep last night?" I asked.

Aunt Lily sighed. "I'm not sure any of us did, sweetie. We took shifts overnight, and there was always someone awake. I don't think that any of us actually slept; more like lay down in bed and try not to worry."

It hadn't occurred to me they would worry about me even if I was staying with them.

"In fact, I'm going home now to report that you are fine and that your guard is doing a good job."

She left and I called Kate into my office and handed her a bag. "Lunch is here."

She smiled. "I was thinking about going out to get us some, but this is great."

As we ate, Kate said, "This is an interesting place. I've never been in here before."

"Thanks. I've recently inherited it, and there's a lot I have to do to rebuild it from the damage."

She looked at me questioningly. "It seems fine in here."

Leaf of Faith

"Most of my supplies are either low or gone, because the shop was trashed the same night Trina was killed."

"I noticed a lot of your supplies were empty, is that normal?"

"Definitely not normal. Trina liked to be fully stocked and ready for anything a customer might need."

"That makes sense. But why do people come here instead of seeing a regular doctor?"

"Different people have different reasons. There are a lot of issues a doctor should treat, but not everything. It's a lot easier on the body to take a ginger syrup for nausea than to take medicine that has side effects, that you have to take more medicine for."

"What would you suggest if I came to you with a headache?" she asked.

"It all depends," I said. "We'd talk for a bit, like you heard me this morning, to see why you had the headache. If it was stress, I'd send you home with a feverfew tincture. If it was a migraine, I'd make you a peppermint oil rub for your temples. Every customer is different."

"And if I kept coming back?" she prompted.

"If you had headaches all the time, I'd send you to your doctor, because you would have something serious that I couldn't help you with.

I'm not a doctor, and Trina stressed that to all our customers."

"Wouldn't you lose money that way?" Kate asked.

"Yes," I said slowly, "we would. If you need something I can't give you, and I tried anyway, I'd still lose your business. Either way I lose sales, but I only lose a client if I lose their trust."

Kate rubbed her temples. "I actually have a headache. What do you suggest?"

I closed my eyes for a moment. "Feverfew for the headache, chamomile tea to relax, and I'd also tell you to get more sleep."

She smiled. "How did you know I haven't been sleeping?"

"The dark circles under your eyes."

Chapter 24

Palmer came to pick me up from work at six.

"Anything?" he asked Kate.

"Customers in and out all day, nothing worth reporting."

"Good. You can go, I'll take over for the night."

I handed Kate a small bag with the feverfew that she refused to take on duty and some chamomile tea. "Thanks for everything."

If Palmer was taking me home, he hadn't found James yet. Probably because he'd fled the state and with any luck, the country. "I don't need to be babysat," I said. "I was safe here all day."

"No way to know if you were safe because Kate was there or not," he said.

I tidied up the counter. "Exactly my point—we'll never know, if she keeps staying with me."

"Ready to go?" he asked.

"I've got more work to do before I can," I said.

"It's been a long day; can it wait until tomorrow?"

"No. Some things have to sit overnight before they're ready. It's about twenty minutes of work, then we can leave."

He frowned as he followed me into the prep room to watch me work. True to my word, I was done in twenty minutes.

"I've got another family dinner at my mother's, and then I'm going to spend the night in my own apartment, in my own bed."

I locked the door and turned to the car parked in front of my shop. At least it wasn't a cruiser this time.

"I've been meaning to say, this is nice for an undercover car," I said.

He opened the passenger door to his Toyota Highlander. "It's my personal car."

I hadn't thought detectives made much money; maybe I was wrong. Or maybe he wasn't above taking a little money on the side.

"Nice for a cop."

"Got it in the divorce settlement," he

muttered.

Well, there was a side of him I'd had no idea about. "Oh, ah, I'm sorry," I flustered. Someday I'd learn how to handle these things gracefully, but apparently that day was not today.

He started the car and didn't say anything else on the short ride to my mother's.

He walked me into the kitchen. "Enjoy dinner and wait for me to take you home."

I blushed at the thought. Another point for me not handling things gracefully.

"Ooooh!" cooed Thea, grinning mischievously. "Going home with the detective?"

It was his turn to be flustered. He turned even redder than me. "That's not what I meant. I'll drive her to her apartment, and then go to my own home. Like a gentleman."

Weird, that statement. Who worried about being a gentleman these days? Pretty much no one, that's who. Maybe the divorce had him sworn off women. That would be a shame.

I glared at Thea. "Shut up," I said before turning to him. "I'll call when I'm ready to go."

"Good. Until we find Trina's killer, I want you to call me anytime you think you should. I'll always take your call."

I smiled as he left the kitchen. Maybe divorce hadn't totally ruined him for other women. Further research was clearly needed.

Palmer paused in the doorway. "I almost forgot. I checked Frank's alibi, or lack of it. He was at the ER. He had been worked over and was getting bandaged up the night Trina was killed."

No wonder Aunt Lily's protection spell hurt him so much. If he already had cracked ribs, that spell would have hurt him much more than she intended.

"Any idea who beat him up?" I asked.

"I've got a few leads, but nothing solid. I'm looking into that now," he said. As he closed the door, he added, "Call me."

I knew everyone was expecting me to spend the night again, but I couldn't, not now. It wouldn't be long before Thea and Delia started using their new powers, and I felt helpless, knowing there was nothing I could do to help Delia. She chose an unsuitable focus, and there was nothing we could do to help. Hopefully, in seven years she'd do better with her next choice. Rather than tell them in advance I was leaving, I snuck into the kitchen after dinner, called Palmer, and waited for him there.

My mother came into the kitchen after a few minutes to check on me. "I thought you might be brewing up a new potion," she said.

I sighed. "Don't get mad at me. I'm going home once Detective Palmer gets here to drive me."

She sat next to me. "That's not safe, is it?"

I shook my head. "I've already doubled the wards on the apartment. Abby and I will be fine. I promise. I need to be in my own bed tonight, and I feel bad for Delia. I wish there was some way to help her."

My mother gave my hand a quick squeeze. "I may have overstated the problem with her. Delia won't achieve her usual level of success with this focus, and sometimes her spells will go wrong. She'll be fine, I promise, and we'll work with her over the coming years to help her find the right next focus."

We were all talented witches in our family, and we were used to having things work out for us. It was tough to maintain an even keel and not show off, because sometimes our talents were amazing.

"I want to find some potion to help the situation; maybe there's one?"

"Be careful—potions to increase ability are banned, and for good reason. It's too easy to abuse them and they can be horribly addicting. It's better to go without them."

Banned potions. Not something I wanted to get involved with. Trina had stressed every day of my apprenticeship that potions designed to make one person better than another were not to be sold or even made in her shop. She was strictly a healing potion person and anything else was forbidden.

"I'm going to do some research, don't worry. I'll check with . . ."

I was going to say I would check with Trina before I made any. My heart sank and I felt the ache of missing my friend. I didn't have a mentor anymore. I was on my own.

"I'll be careful, I promise."

There was a knock on the door. My mother opened it. "Good evening, Detective. Come to take my daughter home?"

He flushed. "Yes, ma'am."

I stood up. "Good. Let's go." The sooner I was out of there, the better. I could have used a good walk to clear my head and get my emotions in check, but I doubted he'd let that happen.

Outside he said, "You don't look well."

I frowned. "Thanks. I just want to go back to my place and relax."

"I get it, sometimes too much family togetherness isn't a good thing."

There was no way I was going to explain my family to him, so I let his comment go. I rested my head on the seat and closed my eyes once I got into his car.

"You don't have to talk about it, if you don't want to. Detectives are trained to be good listeners though," he said.

"Different day, same problem. They want me to stay at home."

Not a lie, honestly. Just not what was bothering me at the moment.

"I understand."

We spent the rest of the ride listening to music. Who knew he liked smooth jazz? I never would have guessed.

"I'm going to walk you into your apartment," he said in a tone that gave no room for argument. I wouldn't have argued anyway, not with James still free.

"You never told me—did you find James?" I asked as we walked up to my second-floor apartment.

"We've got some solid leads, all of which are out of state, and that's the only reason I'm okay with you coming home for the night."

Great. Another person who wanted to tell me how to live my life. At least he had a better reason than my family.

When we got to my apartment, the door was open. Even though I told Abby not to leave the door open or unlocked, she still did. "Abby?" I called out.

I'd never told her I cast wards on the apartment. I tried talking her into an alarm system, which would require the door to be shut. She said no, because she felt that if you weren't safe where you lived, maybe you should live somewhere else. I supposed I'd grow up feeling safe and invulnerable, if I had four football linebackers as brothers too.

Palmer grabbed my arm to stop me from moving further into the apartment. I turned on him, about to give him a piece of my mind. My words died in my throat as I peeked over his shoulder.

Chapter 25

The kitchen chair was knocked over, and Abby's bag had spilled on the living room floor. "Abby!" I yelled again.

I turned to Palmer, who had a gun in his hand. Where had that come from? He must have had it under his jacket, and I hadn't noticed. "Go into the hall and call 911 for backup," he whispered.

I was too frightened to argue. I walked to the end of the hallway and dialed 911.

After a minute, he came out into the hall and motioned for me to join him. "Is she . . ." I started.

He shook his head. "There's no one in the apartment. Does she usually leave the door open?"

"More than I want her to. She's got a bad habit of that. She doesn't knock chairs over or dump her bag out on the floor though."

Two uniforms ran up the stairs silently and stopped near Palmer.

"Seems like a missing person, possible abduction. This is the roommate," Palmer told them.

The short woman officer asked me questions about Abby while writing down everything I said. Palmer and the other officer went into my apartment.

Who would want to take Abby? Her family didn't have money or power. What did they want? I leaned up against the wall for support.

"Miss? Perhaps we should get you inside to sit down," the female officer said.

"Can't. The chair is knocked over."

"You have a couch?" she asked.

I nodded.

"I'm sure that will do." She guided me to the couch and told me to sit.

She conferred with Palmer, then rummaged around in the kitchen. A couple minutes later, she brought me a steaming mug of tea. "Hope you like tea."

I took a sip. There was too much milk and honey in it.

The officer sat next to me. Her nametag

read "Collins." "Now, I don't want you to get upset, but I want you to think over the past couple days. Is there anyone who would want to hurt your roommate?"

I shook my head and took another sip. "Do you think James did this?"

"James who?" Collins asked.

She had no idea what had been going on with me over the last couple days. "It's a long story. He's a guy who drugged me and tried to get me to sign my business over to him."

Her eyes went wide. "Palmer, can you come out here? She thinks it might be some guy named James. Ring any bells to you?"

Palmer left Abby's room and walked into the living room. "He's most likely out of the state. We've been looking for him all day. He'd have tripped our radar if he'd showed up here."

"Was she . . ." I trailed off.

I couldn't ask if she'd been hurt. He seemed to know what I meant. "No signs of a struggle. We can be thankful she doesn't seem to have left the apartment injured."

I took another sip of tea, willing the warm liquid to soothe my growing fears.

Palmer sat on the couch next to me. I tried to hold myself together, but a tear slid down my cheek, followed by another, and then I was sobbing into my tea.

"I'm going to get Kate to come here for the night," he said.

I was relieved. I couldn't face my family right now. "Okay. As long as I can stay here."

He put his hand on my shoulder and gave it a quick pat. "Drink up your tea because I need your help."

If there was anything to say to a witch to get her focused and in action, it would be "I need your help." That went double for my family. I took a deep breath, held it, and tried to release my tension as I exhaled. I couldn't truly relax until we'd found Abby.

I set my mug down. "What do you need?"

"We've had your apartment under surveillance for most of the day, hoping to catch James. We've got a photo of everyone who came in and out. I'd like you to review them and tell me if there's anyone you don't recognize."

He unlocked his phone and pulled up an email. We flipped through the attached photos, and I saw my neighbors, the mailman, and the FedEx delivery guy. "No one suspicious," I said. "Even the delivery guy left empty handed."

Palmer laced his fingers behind his head. "I noticed that the first time I saw the photos."

"So, if she didn't leave with anyone, and didn't leave alone, she must still be in the building, right?" We could find her in just a few minutes if we went door to door. I jumped up off the couch and grabbed his arm. "Let's go find her!"

"Hang on there," he said as I struggled to get him to stand. "No warrant, no search. I've got rules to work with."

"I don't, and I'm sure that if I explain to my neighbors what happened, they'd be happy to help. Besides, do you really want to wait until you can get a warrant?"

He gave in and let me pull him up. "Okay. If anyone says no, we need to walk away, got it?"

I nodded, not believing anyone in my building would be so cruel.

Our first stop was Mrs. Thompson's apartment. She opened the door. "Good evening, my dear. How can I help you?"

Her apartment smelled like gingerbread, and I wished I was only visiting and could stay for a snack. "Good evening. This is my friend Steve Palmer, we're—"

"Detective Steve Palmer, Portsmouth PD," he interrupted me.

I was hoping to keep him from blabbing and worrying my neighbors.

"Abby's not here, is she?" I asked.

"Oh no, dear. She's not. Is she missing?"

"We're not quite sure. Is it, I mean, would you mind if we took a quick peek inside your apartment?" I asked.

She opened the door. "Of course. I'm glad I dusted today."

Palmer did a quick walk-through before he came back to the door. "Thank you, ma'am. You have a lovely home."

I turned so he wouldn't see me rolling my eyes.

We walked past my apartment and stood in front of the Stanleys' door. Abby and I hardly ever saw them, and I was a bit more nervous about asking to go into their apartment.

"All you have to do is ask if Abby's in the apartment. I can tell if they're lying about her being there," Palmer said.

"Really?"

"You get a feel for it after a few years," he said.

I knocked on the door.

Mrs. Stanley opened the door. Her gray hair was tied back, and she was wearing a full apron over her faded dress. "Yes?" she snapped before her face softened. "Oh, Isabella. It's you."

"Hi, Mrs. Stanley. Abby is missing and I wondered if you'd seen her this afternoon."

She shook her head. "No, I haven't. It's Mr. Stanley's bath day, I'm afraid I haven't even had time to look out the window."

I felt like the worst neighbor. About six months ago, Mr. Stanley had fallen off a ladder and was now paralyzed. Of course she was too busy to see our comings and goings, or to worry about much other than her husband. I made a mental note to stop by with some things from The Fancy Tart once my life wasn't overwhelmingly busy.

"Okay, thank you," I said. "Have a good evening."

"Good luck," she said before closing the door. I heard Mr. Stanley calling for her through the closed door.

I turned to Palmer. "He's paralyzed and they don't get out much."

I led him down the stairs to the first floor. At apartment 1C, I stopped him. "This is Mr. Subramanian, he's the landlord."

"I'll take this one," he said.

Palmer rapped on the door and when Mr. Subramanian opened the door, Palmer already had his shield out. "Police. We may have a missing girl in the building."

Mr. S. saw the worry in my face. "Abby? Oh no."

"I'm afraid so," I said. "Did you hear anything earlier today? Any kind of noise?"

He shook his head. "No, nothing, but I was painting my apartment all morning."

Palmer handed him a card. "Call me at any time if you hear from her or think of anything that might help."

Mr. Subramanian took the card. "Of course."

At this point, Kate hurried into the building. She looked relieved that I was standing there. "I'm all yours, boss. What do you want me to do?"

He smiled at her. What was that all about? In the few days I'd known him, he didn't seem like a person who smiled. Maybe they had something going on between them. I'd have to ask her later on.

"Take Isabella upstairs and stay there for the night. You take all calls, in case someone has a ransom demand," Palmer instructed.

"Are we sure it's a kidnapping?" Kate asked.

"No. It seems likely and I don't want to take any chances," Palmer said.

"And what are you going to do?" I asked Palmer.

"I'm going to check the last two apartments and then head out. A second kidnapping in two days? It's got James written all over it. I'm going to find him tonight."

Kate took my arm in a surprisingly firm grip. "You got it. I'll call if anything happens." She propelled me upstairs in that insistent, yet not-quite-painful way cops had that let you know you weren't getting away with anything, and it was best to go along peacefully.

We met Collins and the other officer on the stairs. "Done with the apartment?" Kate asked.

"Yes. We've dusted for prints and there really wasn't much to go through. You can go in now," Collins said.

Once I returned to the apartment, I righted the chair and put everything back in Abby's bag. I brought the bag to her room. Nothing seemed out of place—her bed was made, things were generally tidy. No clues here.

I walked into the kitchen, where Kate was making tea. "I hope you don't mind that I've made myself at home. I thought tea would be nice."

"I'm good, thanks. I think I'm going to lay down and have a good cry."

I half-hoped Abby had left a clue in my room, but nothing was out of place. I closed my eyes and let my senses expand in the room. I didn't feel anyone strange had been in there. All I got were vague impressions of Collins and the other officer who had been here earlier.

I lay on my bed and pulled up the crocheted afghan my family had made for me before I left home. Each person had made one block, with Grandma making up the rest of them. It wasn't so much enchanted as it was comforting to be wrapped in the work of people who loved me. I sighed and closed my eyes.

Big mistake. Worries and questions came crashing into my brain. What if the kidnapper wanted me instead? That made sense, given James's actions yesterday. What if Abby was no use to them, and they killed her? What if they came for me in the middle of the night? Would Kate be enough to fight off several men? What would I tell Abby's parents? What would I tell my family? What if she wasn't kidnapped, and I was blowing this out of proportion?

Her purse on the floor guaranteed something was wrong, and I should be worried.

My best friend was missing, and I was helpless.

Big, fat tears dripped off my cheeks. What good was being a witch if the people closest to me weren't safe? First Trina, now Abby. Who was next? Grandma? One of the aunts? Probably not, because they were strong, not weak like me. Thea and Delia, though, could be in a lot of trouble if they were next on the target list.

I rolled over and punched my pillow. It wasn't fair. There was no reason I shouldn't be able to live a normal life, like any young woman. In the space of a week and a half, everything had been turned upside down, and I felt like nothing was safe or normal anymore.

"Arrrgh!" I yelled in frustration.

Almost immediately there was a soft knock on my door. "Isabella? Are you okay?" asked Kate.

"Yeah, come on in."

She turned on the light and sat on the side of the bed. "I've been in your shoes."

I doubted she had, and my face must have told her so.

"Do you want to hear why I joined the force?" she asked.

"Sure."

"When I was twelve, my parents were murdered." She had such a matter-of-fact tone that it was heartbreaking.

I sat up, shocked. "Oh, my goddess, Kate. I'm sorry."

"They were the victims of a random home invasion. We don't know what happened, except in the end, my parents were shot."

"You sound so calm. Did they get caught?"

Kate shook her head. "No. Or not yet. I'm calm because I know, eventually, they'll be caught."

"Where were you when this happened?"

"My sister and I were out with our aunt and uncle. We found them when we got home."

How horrible. That would be enough to destroy any little girl's life.

"Police came and promised they'd hunt for

the killers." She sighed. "I'm sure they did. My aunt and uncle tried to shield me from the investigation, so I wasn't kept informed back then. After a year of no progress, I decided that was enough. If they weren't going to solve the crime, then I was going to have to do it myself, and solve all the other crimes they couldn't."

"Wow. That's a lot for a girl to take on herself, and here you are, solving crimes."

She frowned. "I haven't solved any yet. That's why I'm here though. Palmer understands my motivation, and he calls me in when the chief won't let him have more officers. It's like an unofficial duty shift."

"Wait, I'm confused. What's unofficial duty?"

"It's like I'm doing Palmer a favor. I'm not actually on duty, so my powers are limited, but if bad things go down, I've got more latitude for action than your regular civilian."

"Were you on unofficial duty all day with me too?" I asked.

"Yes."

"And you're not getting paid for any of this?"

She shook her head. "I'm not in it for the money. I spent the day with you, and I'd have been insulted if he hadn't called me in to sit with you tonight. And tomorrow, when this becomes an official investigation, I'll be put on it because I'm familiar with the case, and you."

Palmer was doing her a big favor, careerwise. I wished she was getting paid for it though. I knew how tough it could be to do unpaid work but still have to pay all your bills.

"You took your day off to babysit me? I feel like I owe you something."

"Nah. I have a cause in life, and there's nothing money can do for that."

I was amazed. I didn't think people like this existed anymore: selfless people who were interested in the good of others over themselves. This painted Palmer in a different light for me too. He was a man who cared about the people around him, no matter who they were. As long as he wasn't using her to advance his own career, or because they were dating. I had to find out about this.

"So, you and Palmer. Am I wrong, or is there something between the two of you?"

"There's absolutely nothing between us. I get why some women want that male authority figure thing, guy who can help them up the ladder of success. I want success as much as anyone else, and I'll get it with my own abilities. Plus, he's not interested in me."

"Good for you. But are you sure he's not interested in you?"

"He's interested in someone else," she said.

"Really? Who?"

"He's interested in someone else sitting in this room," she said.

He sure didn't seem it. "No way. I'm just an unlucky person who keeps getting in trouble. I'm sure he's only watching out for my safety."

"I think it's more than that. Not that he'd ever tell you, though. At least not while you're part of an ongoing investigation."

She gave a little shrug. "Anyway, are you feeling a little better?"

I wasn't, although having someone to talk to helped. "I'd like to call my cousins," I said.

"Sure. If you get any other calls, make sure to take them. I'll go see if I can make something for dinner. It's going to be a long night and I doubt either of us will get much sleep."

I knew at least one of us would, but I'd need my cousins' help for that.

Chapter 26

I called my cousins, filled them in on the details of my night, and they came right over.

Kate let them in, introduced herself, and returned to the kitchen. I brought my cousins into my room to talk.

"So, what are we going to do?" Delia asked.

"Another midnight all-black recon?" asked Thea.

"I don't know. I'm not sure where to start," I said.

"Obviously, we start with magic. We should be able to find Abby straight away," Thea said.

"Yeah, but what about Kate?" asked Delia.

I frowned. I was beginning to think of her

as a friend, and did friends really give friends sleeping potions? Did that still qualify as protecting someone? What would Grandma say? I didn't dare call her, because if she caught even a small whiff of what we were planning, we'd be in serious trouble.

I walked to my closet and pulled out the small trunk I kept my potions in. I ran my fingers over the magical lock and opened it. "I can take care of her. I've got a couple vials of restful night potion here, and I'll *freshen up* her drink."

"While you're out there, pick up something of Abby's, and I'll try to find out what happened to her," Thea said.

Excellent use of her new talent for psychometry. "I'll grab her purse. It was dumped out on the floor."

"What should I do?" asked Delia.

I froze for a moment, not wanting her to do anything. I was afraid any spell she cast would backfire.

"You can distract Kate so Isabella can dose her," said Thea.

Even though Kate had switched to coffee, it didn't take more than a couple minutes for her to fall soundly asleep on the couch. I grabbed Abby's purse, and Thea looked through it.

"I think I'm getting something from this mirror." Thea closed her eyes and whispered an incantation. After a minute, she snapped her eyes open. "I could hear Abby talking. She was frustrated that someone kept bothering her."

"What did she say?" I asked.

"Something about not being thirsty and she'd see him for his usual eight creams and four sugars. I guess he'd been bothering her all day," Thea said.

I knew exactly who she was annoyed with. The same guy who annoyed me every single day at the bakery. Our downstairs neighbor, Chuck.

"Can you get anything else?"

Thea closed her eyes again and focused on the mirror. "I can see further into the past now. She opened the door, was annoyed with who was there, and then he shoved his way into the apartment. He started talking to her, but I can't make out what he said. She tried to make him leave, instead he pushed her to the dining table. She ran around the end of the table. He sounded furious, and he knocked the chair over to get to her. He yanked her arm, and she dropped her purse, and then—oh no, he pulled her into the hallway." She opened her eyes again. "She's been kidnapped. I didn't see who it was."

"It was Chuck, our downstairs neighbor."

"The one who keeps bothering you at work?" Delia asked.

I nodded. I knew he was a jerk, but

kidnapping? There was one easy way to get to him — bang down the door to his apartment. "Let's go." I headed out, fury coursing through my veins.

"Isabella," cried Delia. "Wait a minute, please. Don't we need a plan?"

I didn't need a plan, not when I knew who had taken her.

Mrs. Thompson was standing in the hallway, almost as though she had been waiting for me. "Where are you going, dear?"

"Chuck has Abby. We're going to his apartment," I growled.

She looked at the three of us. "Good. I'll come."

I didn't think that was a good idea, I mean, she was old, and I didn't want her to get hurt or be in our way. If he was willing to grab a woman out of her apartment for no reason, then who knows what else he might do.

I strode past her. "Go into your apartment, Mrs. Thompson. We've got this handled."

We rushed down the stairs and stopped at Chuck's door. I tried the doorknob. The apartment was locked. I turned to my cousins. "Can either of you hex this door open?" I asked.

"Let me try," said Delia.

I was afraid she would offer to cast a spell. It couldn't hurt though; it wasn't like the door would become even more locked.

"Go for it," I said as I stepped far behind her.

Delia muttered something under her breath and smoke puffed out of the lock. She tried the handle, but the door didn't open.

"You wouldn't mind giving an old lady a chance, would you?" Mrs. Thompson asked.

Apparently, she didn't listen to instructions well.

"Why not," I said.

She walked up to the door, put her hands on the lock and after a moment, tried the handle. The door didn't open.

"What did you do to this lock?" she asked Delia.

"I did a quick opening spell," she said, a bit defensively.

Mrs. Thompson shook her head. "Well, that will never do. We're going to have to brute force the door, ladies." She stood back and called out a louder spell, loud enough that I was worried Chuck would hear us out in the hall. She pulled her hands to the sides of her head and thrust them forward. The door splintered inward and we rushed in.

"Abby, are you here?" I yelled.

We spread out and checked each room in the apartment with no luck. Under Chuck's bed were a pair of Timberland boots, size ten. I picked one up by the lace and looked at the sole. I didn't see oil, but I detected traces of some of our more potent herbs. I dropped the boot and scrambled out of the room.

"What's going on here?" Mr. Subramanian said from the hallway. He poked his head through the doorframe and looked stunned. "Did you blow up the door?" he asked.

I smiled what I hoped was my most convincing smile. "That would be weird, wouldn't it? We were walking by to go out, and this happened . . . ." I paused as though to think for a moment. "You don't let Chuck keep explosives in the apartment, do you?"

He walked in. "Chuck, are you here?"

We knew there would be no answer; the apartment was empty.

"Of course I don't let tenants keep explosives in the apartments. Don't be ridiculous. Let's go back out into the hall."

We walked out of the apartment. "You don't know where Chuck is right now, do you?" I asked.

Mr. Subramanian shook his head. "No. He asked for the key to the empty apartment, though. He said he wanted to see it now that most of the renovations are done. He said he might want to change apartments. I was coming to get the key from him when I heard all this ruckus."

That must be where he was hiding Abby. "Maybe he's there. Do you have another key for the door?"

Mr. Subramanian took a large key ring from his pocket and held up a key. "I'll look for him."

There was no way I was going to let him check the apartment without me. I followed him, heart pounding out of my chest, hoping it wasn't too late to find Abby.

He unlocked the door—so much easier than trying to blow it up—and walked in. "Chuck?" he called out. Again there was no answer.

We fanned out through all the rooms. The newly painted and decorated apartment was lovely; I could see why Chuck might want to move in.

I thought this was a dead end, but then I saw it. Abby's necklace was hanging on the shower spigot. She had been here and had been able to leave us a message.

"Thea, come here," I yelled.

"Yeah? Any luck?" she asked.

I pointed to the necklace. I hadn't wanted to pick it up, because I didn't want to taint any imagery that might have been attached to it. "That's Abby's necklace."

Thea picked it up by the chain and

dropped it.

"What's wrong?" I asked.

"It's bad. Really bad."

Mr. Subramanian joined us, and I slipped the necklace into my back pocket. "I guess he's not here either. He was, though, because he was using the kitchen."

"Show me," I said.

Trina's file of missing potions was scattered on the kitchen counter, along with small bags of potion ingredients. "What is this nonsense?" he asked. "Was Chuck trying to make these recipes?"

I picked up the sheet of paper closest to the stove, labeled "LOVE POTION – ILLEGAL TO OWN, MAKE, USE" and when Mr. Subramanian turned around, I passed it to Mrs. Thompson.

Her eyes widened. She folded the paper up and tucked it into her waistband with the swiftness of movement that told me she was used to the sneaky life. Delia collected the rest of the papers and held them behind her back.

"Why did you need to talk to him? Is it about Abby? You should let the police find her," Mr. Subramanian said.

"It's nothing important," I said. "I'll catch him another time. Thanks for your help."

The four of us walked out of the apartment and down the hall, away from Mr. Subramanian's door.

"Cool door blasting," Delia said to Mrs. Thompson once we'd closed the door to my apartment.

"Thank you." She turned to me. "Now, who's going to tell me what's going on here?"

I nodded to Thea, who told her about the vision she had from the mirror.

"Psychometry witch, that will come in handy," she said.

"Isabella found Abby's necklace in the bathroom of the empty apartment too." Delia said.

I pulled it out of my pocket and handed it to Thea.

After an excruciatingly long minute, Thea opened her eyes. "Okay, I've seen enough. He was ranting and raving at Abby—I couldn't understand all of it. He's in love with Abby and thinks if they spent more time together, she'd fall in love with him too."

"That would make sense, given the potion he was trying to brew up." Mrs. Thompson pulled the sheet out and handed it to me. "Trina should have known better than to have these," she said.

I frowned. "I had no idea she did. I thought I knew everything about the business, but I had no idea what Trina was up to."

I turned to Thea. "Where did they go?"

"Chuck noticed the plainclothesman

watching the house and freaked out. First, he brought her to the empty apartment because the windows are covered with plastic, then he got more nervous and decided they had to leave."

"How did they leave if the house was being watched?" I asked.

Thea closed her eyes and ran a finger over the top of the locket. "I think he gave her something to make her do what he wanted, another potion I think, because it's hard to see what's going on now."

"Oh bats," I said. "We've got to go. We can't wait around here, because we don't know what will happen if he tries to use more potions."

"May I see the locket?" Mrs. Thompson asked.

Thea handed her the locket, and she closed her eyes, mumbling a spell. The chain grew taut in her hand, the locket pointing straight down to the floor.

"There is another way out of the building," said Mrs. Thompson.

"Where?" Thea asked.

"The bulkhead from the basement. It leads out to the woods behind the building. You can't see it from the street, so they might have snuck out there."

"What was that spell?" I asked.

"It's a location spell. We'll use it to track

her until we find her. Follow me."

I was in awe. I had no idea there was such a spell. If Mrs. Thompson hadn't been with us, what would we have done? Thea couldn't see more from the locket, Delia's spellcasting was not trustworthy, and I'd already run out of ideas. "Mrs. Thompson," I said.

"Yes, dear?"

"Thank you for your help. If you hadn't been here, I'm not sure what we'd have done."

She stopped at the door to the basement. "We don't work alone, and we never let one of our own get into any more trouble than is necessary."

We work together. This was the entire message my family was trying to hammer into me. Somehow, it made more sense coming from Mrs. Thompson. Together, we could make things happen that would be impossible for one person.

Could I do this? Could I continue to work with my family and still keep my fledgling independence? It was probably time to talk to the aunts about this.

Behind the building, Mrs. Thompson pointed to the dirt at the bulkhead. "One set of footprints, but deep. My guess is that he was carrying Abby rather than trying to drag her along."

She followed the footsteps to the grass and then walked to the trees, following the tug of the locket. We followed behind her, single file, until we reached the paved playground the small copse bordered.

We stepped out of the trees, not sure what to do next. I jogged to the front of the school, scanning the street for the two of them or for his beat-up car. I saw nothing.

I looked around again, frantic for any sign of Abby and Chuck, but there were no clues.

The necklace continued to pull toward the sidewalk, and we followed, each of us with one eye glued on the locket and one eye hoping to see him in the evening traffic, desperate for any sign of Abby.

Chapter 27

Three blocks from the house, Chuck's green Chevy Cruze pulled behind the 7-Eleven and the necklace changed orientation to match. My heart leapt—we'd just found Abby. I ducked behind a car parked on the side of the road and motioned for everyone else to do as I did.

"It's Chuck, he's behind the store," I said.

Chuck came sauntering around the building, whistling like he didn't have a care in the world. Once he was in the store, I told Mrs. Thompson to call Palmer while the rest of us went inside to confront him.

She put the necklace in her pocket and dialed 911 as we ran across the street and into the store. Chuck was just tall enough that we could see his hair above the shelves that filled the store.

I found him in the back corner, picking up a six-pack of beer. Ugh. How typical. "Where's Abby?"

He flinched and turned around, surprise on his face to see the three of us. "How should I know?"

"She's missing, and you have her. Tell me where she is," I demanded.

He tried to push past me in the narrow aisle, but with Thea and Delia behind me, he didn't get far.

"Get out of my way," he growled.

When we didn't, he turned and walked down the aisle, away from the door. When he rounded the corner, he made a break for the door, knocking Mrs. Thompson down on her side. She grabbed his leg and he fell next to her, dropping the beer.

Mrs. Thompson had given us just enough time to catch up to him. I sat on his chest, and when he tried to rise, Thea and Delia sat on his legs, keeping him pinned to the floor.

"Hey, what's going on over there," the cashier barked at us.

Mrs. Thompson got up. "Nothing to worry about, Stu. I've already called the police, and they'll be here in a couple minutes."

At the word "police," Chuck redoubled his efforts to dislodge us. He started rolling and almost succeeded when Stu came over. Stu was a tall guy who looked like he played linebacker at Portsmouth High.

"Let me take care of him, ladies," Stu said. He grabbed the collar of Chuck's shirt and pulled him up. "You're not making trouble for Mrs. Thompson, are you?" he said as he dragged Chuck to the counter.

Delia flipped the door sign to "closed" and stayed there to keep any other customers from coming in.

Thea and I followed Stu, and Mrs. Thompson whispered something I could not hear. Stu brought Chuck behind the counter and zip-tied him to a waist-high metal shelf that was bolted into the wall. Once Stu finished, his face slackened and his eyes closed.

Chuck looked at us and cringed. "No! Don't make me," he babbled.

I had no idea what was going on with him, so I turned to Mrs. Thompson and was shocked to see Trina's ghost behind her.

"It's a projection, and Stu is in a trance. He won't remember any of this, and he won't move until I release him." Mrs. Thompson whispered to me.

Projections are hard, at least for younger witches like me and my cousins. I was amazed how easily Mrs. Thompson could create one.

I decided to play it up to get Chuck to confess. "Why are you afraid of Trina? Will she tell us something you don't want anyone to know?"

Chuck squatted behind the counter and tried to make himself as small as possible. "Get her out of here!" he yelled.

"You think she's a vengeful spirit? Tell me, what revenge would Trina want on you?" Mrs. Thompson asked.

He'd begun rocking back and forth, to the extent his zip-tied arms would let him.

"Can you make her talk?" I asked Mrs. Thompson.

The image of Trina pointed at Chuck. "Tell them what you did."

He whimpered but said nothing.

"Tell them!" Trina's ghost screamed.

"I didn't mean to. Please don't kill me," he said, crying and sniffling.

Thea grabbed a box of tissues from a shelf and opened it. She walked behind the counter, sat next to Chuck and handed him a tissue. "It will be okay, as long as you tell us what happened." She put a hand on his arm. "The truth is always best. You can tell us and we can make sure Trina never hurts you."

Chuck lifted his head up and took the tissue. He blew his nose and cautiously peeked over the counter. He snapped his head down and whispered, "She's still there."

"She'll go once you tell the truth, I promise."

Chuck took a ragged breath and began to confess. "I didn't mean to hurt her—it just all got out of hand. She kept saying she didn't have what I needed. I didn't believe her. Finally, she told me she had the ingredients outside in the greenhouse. Once we got outside, she yelled her head off, and I panicked. I panicked and hit her with a rock." He put his head in his hands and started crying. "I didn't mean to . . ."

Delia shushed him. "Chuck, where is Abby?"

"Trunk. Out back," he wailed.

Thea and I ran out to Chuck's car. I felt around for the latch and popped the trunk open.

Abby's body lay there and I let out a cry. "Abby! Oh goddess, Abby!"

She rolled her head toward me and smiled.

I pulled her from the car and hugged her with everything I had. She was alive. "Are you okay?" I asked, looking her over for any injuries.

"Isabella?"

"Yes, sweetie. It's me. Don't worry, you're safe with me now."

She frantically turned her head. "Where's Chuck? We're going to spend the rest of our lives together."

I sighed. He had given her the love potion after all. "He's inside, sweetie, but listen. I think this is temporary, and you might change your mind by the morning."

"No way. He's my soulmate," Abby sighed.

"Let's go into the store and find him," I suggested, hoping Mrs. Thompson would be able to reverse the potion's effects. If not, we'd have to go to Grandma, and then there'd be a lot of explaining to do. Mrs. Thompson was our only hope.

When we returned to the store, the image of Trina had vanished, and Chuck was still sobbing. Abby ran to him and put her arms around him. "It's okay, we'll get through whatever this is," she cooed. Then she noticed the zip ties. "What? Why? What have you done to him? Cut these off immediately," she demanded.

I turned to Mrs. Thompson. "Can you help her?"

"I can fix this only temporarily. The permanent fix needs to come from a potion that you'll have to make." She raised her arms. "Take this child and make her whole, undo the harm to her heart and mind, cleanse her of the potion and let her see the light."

She stood in front of Stu and snapped her fingers. He blinked and shook his head.

"It's okay, Stu. The police will be here any minute now."

Abby looked at Chuck before realizing she had her arm around him. "What?" She took several steps back. "Chuck? Did you try to rob the store?" She turned around and saw the rest of us on the other side of the counter. "Hey, uh," she said as she rubbed her head. "What's going on?"

I grabbed her hand and gave it a squeeze. "We're not sure, but we think he gave you a new kind of club drug, like a roofie. You may not remember everything quite right, or even at all."

Her jaw dropped. "He did what?"

"Don't worry. Palmer will be here any second and then Chuck will be taken away."

As if on cue, Palmer and a patrol officer entered the store and walked to us, his eyes finally landing on the zip-tied Chuck. "What in the world . . ."

"This is Abby's kidnapper," Mrs. Thompson said.

"This true?" he asked Abby.

Abby broke out into tears, the reality of what was going on finally seeming to hit her. "Yes," she whispered.

"He's also got boots in his apartment the same size as the print you found in the apothecary office," I said.

"I don't even want to know how you found

that out," he said.

Palmer cut the zip ties, only to replace them with handcuffs. He handed Chuck to the patrol officer. "Read him his rights and bring him to the station."

Palmer turned toward us, frowning. I'm sure he was upset with us, but we'd found Abby, so how mad could he really be?

"This your roommate?" he asked.

I nodded. "She's been drugged, so I don't think you're going to get much out of her tonight."

Thea, Delia, Mrs. Thompson, and I walked out of the store and Palmer took my arm and led me to the side of the building. "I could arrest you."

"For what?"

"Interfering with an investigation, false imprisonment, and generally not doing what I tell you."

I smiled up at him. "I hardly think not doing what you tell me is illegal."

"If Kate hadn't called me to tell me you'd all snuck out, I might not have gotten here in time. What if something had happened, and Chuck got loose?"

Kate. I'd forgotten all about her. How was I going to explain what had happened to her? Was I any better than Chuck if I slipped her a sleeping potion? We both used potions to get people to do what we wanted them to.

My head began to spin and Palmer put an arm around me to hold me up. "Hey, it's okay. Abby's safe now. You're safe now."

I gazed into his dark brown eyes and knew I couldn't explain. There was no way to convince him my motives were good, whereas Chuck's were bad. We'd both done something wrong.

I turned and retched on Chuck's car, my tea coming up, bitter like the realization that I couldn't always trust my actions or motives.

"We've got her," Delia said to Palmer as the ambulance pulled up. "You take Abby to the hospital. We'll follow in a few minutes."

He walked Abby toward the ambulance.

"What was that all about?" asked Thea. "Suddenly you went pale as the moon and looked like you were going to pass out."

"Kate," I whispered. "The sleeping potion. Tell me how that's any better than what Chuck did to Abby, or what James did to me." My heart clenched with guilt.

Delia frowned. "I see what you mean."

Mrs. Thompson, however, did not. "Don't be a fool. You put Kate to sleep to keep her safe and out of harm's way. Both James and Chuck used drugs to get what wasn't theirs. There's a world of difference, and the fact that you are upset thinking there isn't is a good sign. You keep examining your motives like this, and you won't go astray."

I wasn't sure if I believed her, but I felt a little reassured that another witch thought I didn't do the wrong thing.

"Although, examining your motives before your actions is a better way to go about it all. You'll have to do that from now on," Mrs. Thompson said.

Think before acting. Someday I'd remember to do that.

We rejoined Palmer by his car, where the officer was filling him in. "Chuck's confirmed what you told me. He was never on our radar for Trina's killer. He feels guilty, too, seems to think he's being haunted by Trina's ghost."

"It sounds like you're saying without us, you never would have caught him," I said.

Palmer coughed. "I never say that to civilians. Makes them think they can go around playing Nancy Drew with no consequences. And the four of you won't be doing that, will you?"

I opened my eyes wide, pretending innocence. "Detective Palmer, I don't know what you mean. We called you as soon as we thought anything was wrong."

"Ha," he huffed. "If you think I'm falling for that, you've got another thing coming. Can I trust the three of you to go directly home, or do I need Kate to escort you?"

Wait, three of us? "Where's Mrs. Thompson?"

"I sent her with the ambulance. She hit her head when Chuck knocked her down, and she was getting a big egg on her forehead," Thea said.

"And what were you thinking?" Palmer's eyes flashed and my pulse quickened. "Bringing a little old lady out on some stupid hunt for a man who turns out to be a killer? He could have killed all of you."

"First of all, Detective, if you'd done your job right, he wouldn't have been free to kidnap Abby in the first place. Second of all, we weren't in any real danger here. There were four of us to one of him. We had him pinned to the floor, and he wasn't going anywhere."

Palmer swung his head up and looked me straight in the eye. "Promise me you won't pull a stunt like this again."

A witch's word was her bond, but we're a crafty bunch, and I seriously doubted Abby would be kidnapped again. "Absolutely. I promise," I said.

"Good. Now go home. You'll need to give statements in the morning."

Chapter 28

We weren't able to keep Chuck's arrest and our part in it from Grandma and the aunts. Two hours after we got back to my apartment, they were there.

"Do you know what could have happened to you?" each of the aunts asked her daughter at some point during the grueling interrogation.

Thea, Delia, and I finally gave in and told them the whole story: why Chuck murdered Trina, how Mrs. Thompson helped us when we needed it, and how we were never in any danger at all.

"Tell that to Abby," Grandma said.

I thought she was being unfair. Thea, Delia and I were never going to be kidnapped; only Abby was in danger.

"And don't forget what happened to you," my mother said.

"That was completely unrelated to Abby's kidnapping," I said. "It's not my fault James drugged me."

"Still, I want you to move home, immediately," she demanded.

I expected this. "No. There's no way I'm leaving Abby alone here. There's no way I'm leaving my best friend when she'll need support." And then I hit her with my best line: "You didn't raise me to abandon my obligations. Besides, there's nothing to say Aunt Lily's prophecy was even about me. All it said was keep your children close. Maybe it meant you need to stay close to Grandma."

She frowned at me. "Possibly. But it might be a long time before we figure it out."

They left before Abby came home, shepherded by her parents.

Mr. Allen was serious at all times, and even more tonight. His white eyebrows furrowed and he loomed over me, as though the events of the day were my fault. "She won't listen to me and refuses to spend even one night at home, so I insisted I come and check the security of the building."

He walked around, checking the windows and the door locks.

Mrs. Allen, no less protective but much less intimidating than her husband, said, "Isabella, dear, we're grateful that you found her." She gave me a hug and sniffled.

"It's okay, Chuck's confessed and I'm sure he'll go to jail for a long time," I reassured her.

At least I hoped so. I planned to talk to Mrs. Thompson about making it seem like he was haunted if he ever came near Abby again. That, more than anything else, would keep her safe.

She went into the kitchen. "Why don't I make us some tea? I think we can all use some to settle our nerves."

"I'm going to talk to your landlord. I don't like this door. It seems too easy to break down," Mr. Allen said.

Abby rolled her eyes. "It's going to be like this for a while, then they'll calm down. They always do."

She was right. She never got into any serious trouble growing up, and by now we could practically predict when her overprotective parents would stop worrying. I hugged her. "If you're not happy here anymore, or if you don't want to live here, we can move. It's completely understandable, and I wouldn't blame you a bit for wanting to never see this apartment again."

Abby took the mug of tea her mother made and sat on the couch. "I thought about that. I don't want to run from my problems. Besides, we know all the other people in the building, and I feel safer with my neighbors—well, the ones who aren't Chuck, anyway—than I would with a bunch of strangers."

I nodded. That's the best friend I knew—never one to back down from a challenge, or to avoid facing her fears.

After several awkward hours of questions about the day, Abby's parents finally left to go home for the night. Abby relaxed onto the couch. "Finally. Look, if you don't mind, I'm going to take a quick shower and go to bed."

I gave her another big hug. "Go. Do what you think is best. I'll be here if you need me. And don't feel bad if you want to talk in the middle of the night. I'm here."

Giving a statement is boring. Going over every single detail again and again made me wonder if Palmer didn't think we were suspects somehow too.

It's a good thing Thea, Delia and I spent an hour after we woke up going over our stories and making sure they were the same, yet different enough so that Palmer didn't think we had rehearsed.

Mrs. Thompson was still under observation, and Palmer hadn't been able to question her yet. Thea, who was the first of us to be questioned, went straight over to talk to Mrs. Thompson once her interview was over.

During my interview, I let it slip that Frank stopped by to mention he was going to make a new start by paying off his bookie and moving far away. I didn't want to tell him everything I knew; he could work for the details. In return, he told me James and Mick, the sleazy bartender, had been picked up in Boston. Mick had been charged with possession of Rohypnol, and he'd already implicated James. They were both looking at felony assault charges and would spend some time in jail. When I finished with my interview, I went to the apothecary, hours late, but at least it wasn't a full day gone.

I opened the door and breathed in the lavender and lilac scents that permeated the air. I felt more at peace now, knowing Chuck had been arrested and Trina's spirit could rest peacefully.

Before I let in customers, I went to the greenhouse and closed my eyes, thinking about Abby and the potion Chuck had made her. Immediately the antidote sprang to mind. Skunk cabbage and yarrow, with peppermint and honey to help make it taste a bit less repulsive.

I cut a few leaves of each and brewed them on the small hot plate in the greenhouse. There was no way I wanted the shop to smell like skunk cabbage.

Once the water came to a boil, I poured the tea into a travel mug and quickly put the lid on it. I knew my potion would remove any effects of the love potion Chuck gave Abby yesterday, because all he could do was put ingredients together. The intention I added after my anti-love spell was finished would make sure she returned to her normal feelings for him.

Abby had the day off, and I'd asked her to meet me when she was done with Palmer. She walked in and held up a paper bag from The Fancy Tart. "Guess what I've got?"

I put my hand to my head as though I could see through the bag. "Two éclairs. The real question, though, is am I going to have to share them?"

She laughed. "Of course you do." She rubbed her temples. "Damn. Whatever Chuck gave me has a serious hangover."

I looked at her, trying to see if any of the love potion's effects were returning. She didn't have a haze of magic around her, so it looked like the potion had worn off quickly. I handed her the cup of tea. "I have just the thing. You have to drink it all, so it's best to go fast. Come to the office and have a seat."

Abby wrinkled her nose. "This is one of those medicinal things, isn't it?"

I smiled. "Drink it, then you can eat the éclair, and you'll wash the taste right out of your mouth."

She frowned, and did as I asked.

"Oh!" she said while gagging. "That's hideous."

"Éclair," I said, handing it to her.

She took a huge bite of hers and swallowed. "If I didn't know better, I'd think you were trying to poison me. Was that . . . skunk in there?"

I smiled. "It's only skunk cabbage. How do you feel now?"

She took another bite. "The headache is gone."

"And how do you feel about Chuck?"

She sat up and took a much smaller bite of her pastry. "I had planned to visit him, now I don't want to. My parents wanted me to be all angry at him. Last night I refused. Today, though, I'm ready to press every charge there is and then some."

"That's my girl. Go home, call Palmer, and then tell your parents. They'll be glad you're doing the right thing."

Leaf of Faith

I escorted her out of the shop and hung the open sign. I snapped my finger to light Trina's memorial candle. "I got him, Trina, and everything is going to be okay."

I've never been a person who has any sensitivity to ghosts, but there couldn't be any other explanation for the flicker of the candle flame, or the heart-shaped smoke that formed above her photo.

The End

Excerpt of What in Carnation

Book 2 of the Isabella Proctor Cozy Mystery series

It had been three months since I inherited the business from my mentor and friend, Trina Bassett after her murder by a man who was obsessed with, and had kidnapped my best friend, Abby.

I'd been working hard all morning and I needed a break. I grabbed my mug and walked out to the sales floor to the complimentary tea station for more caffeine.

Today's tea was mango matcha, and I'd instituted having a caffeinated and decaf pot available for customers. I poured more of the caffeinated in my mug and stirred in a dollop of honey. Goddess give me strength to deal with it all. I asked John if he could choose new suppliers for me, but he laughed. There was no way he could choose quality - he could only choose the cheapest. We agreed we didn't necessarily want that. My customers deserved better.

Leaf of Faith

I loved my customers to pieces and they made all this work worth it. Mrs. Newcomb's raspy cough seemed to be clearing up with her new potion and lately I'd noticed an uptick in first-time customers. Hopefully, in a week or two, many of them would return to be second-time and then long-term customers.

The door chimes rang and Agatha walked in. Agatha was the only client I felt like I'd failed. Her brown hair was matted and she was wearing mismatched shoes. Her blouse was half-tucked into loose jeans that hung low on her hips, telling me she hadn't been eating enough. The voice in her head, Alice, must be strong. "Good afternoon, Agatha. How are you?" I said.

She walked straight to the tea station and poured herself a mug of decaf. "Horrible."

I said nothing because I knew she'd continue as long as I didn't interrupt.

"Alice is angry that I keep trying to shut her up and sometimes she won't let me take my medicine. She makes me dump it out instead." She looked from her mug to me, tears welling in her eyes. "I try not to, but she's stronger than me and when she doesn't let me sleep I don't have the strength to stop her."

I put my hand on her shoulder. "Oh, Agatha, that's terrible."

She took a sip of her tea. "I don't know what to do and I feel like giving up. Just let her have the body so I can sleep and not fight for every single thing."

My heart broke for her. I hadn't been able to find a potion that did more than keep some of her symptoms at bay. Honestly, treating mental illness was far outside my abilities but she refused to get help anywhere else.

"Maybe it's time to go see my friend, Dr. Rebecca." I held my hands up to forestall her objections. "I know you don't want to, but there's nothing more I can do for you."

Rebecca Cleary was a local psychiatrist I'd called when I realized my potions couldn't cure Agatha. She wasn't happy about Agatha relying on potions and wanted me to bring her in for a consultation. I didn't want to nag Agatha, because as far as I knew, I was the only person watching her mental health. If she stopped coming to see me, I wasn't sure she'd have anyone in her life to care about her.

"You know Alice won't let me."

"Please. I'll come with you and make sure nothing bad happens. All we have to do is talk to the doctor for a little bit. You don't have to take any other medicine, just talk."

Agatha shook her head and banged her mug down on the tea table. "I need my meds, then I have to go."

I sighed. "Okay. But take the first dose here, where I can see you." I'd instituted this rule with her months ago, hoping it would get her back on the path to regular doses. Given the way she looked today, it didn't seem to be working. Before I gave her the bottle, I closed my eyes and used my intuition to make sure the potion I'd made for her was still the right one. All I saw was ashwagandha, which was what was waiting for her behind the counter.

My intuition guided me to make the appropriate potions for people. I closed my eyes, thought about the person and then I would see what they needed. I'd made one potion for my grandma without having her with me and it had made her hallucinate. Now I always made sure to check my work with the person in the room.

She rubbed her hands on her pants. "Fine. Whatever."

"Great. It's waiting for you back at the register."

We walked to the back of the shop and I pulled her bottle out from under the counter. I opened it and held it out to her with a plastic spoon. "Two spoonfuls."

She frowned but took the spoon and bottle. She poured one spoon and took it, then the second. "There. Are you happy now?"

"I am. I worry about you. I'm afraid some day Alice is going to hurt you."

She took the cap from my hand and screwed it onto her bottle. "So am I," she whispered before she fled the building.

I rested my head in my hands, wishing there was anything else I could do. I'd already talked to Grandma and the aunts, but even though they were more experienced witches than me, they didn't have nearly as much potions knowledge and had no other suggestions.

Leaf of Faith

The next nearest potion witch I knew of was in Sewell but I hadn't had time to visit her yet. I was going to have to make that a priority. Maybe I could talk Agatha in to coming with me for a consultation.

I looked out the picture window, watching people walk by and was surprised to see Caroline Arneson staring through the window at me. She had been standing outside the apothecary intermittently for the last month or so. I didn't know why, maybe she was trying to intimidate me?

Agatha hadn't paid me. In fact, she hadn't paid me for weeks. I took ten dollars out of my pocket and rang up the transaction. My accountant would have a fit if he knew I was doing this, but we'll just keep this a secret.

I was about to go back to my computer and hundred open tabs when my neighbor, Mrs. Thompson, walked into the store. Without her, we might never have caught the man who killed Trina and kidnapped Abby, my best friend. Since that horrible week this past March, Mrs. Thompson and I had been having tea together a couple times a week. She invited me over at what seemed to be the most random times for a chat. She was a witch, too, although she never told me much about herself. All I knew was that she could track and find people with her magic. She wanted to know about me, my plans, and what I saw myself doing in the future. Some days I felt like I was in a month-long interview for an unnamed job.

My future seemed pretty set in stone to me - run the apothecary, learn as much as I could about potionmaking, and help people whenever I could.

She never seemed satisfied with that answer, but didn't hint about what else she might want to hear. She also played a mean game of cribbage and more than once I wondered if her cards were marked, or if she used magic to win. The number of twenty-four-point hands she got was ridiculous.

Today she was dressed in seersucker Capri pants, boat shoes, and a blue polo shirt. She looked like any other gray-haired grandmother out shopping, but I knew better. She had a sharp mind and a dry sense of humor.

"Hey, Mrs. T., how are you?" I asked as she approached the counter I was standing at.

"Just fine, Miss P."

Leaf of Faith

She'd asked me to call her Mary, but I didn't feel right about it. She was my elder, and Grandma had made sure we all respected our elders, particularly those who were witches. In retaliation, she called me Miss P. rather than Isabella. I could live with that.

I looked on my shelf of prepared potions under the counter, but there were none with her name. "Are you here to pick something up?" I asked.

"Oh, no, dear. Jameson is doing fine. Whatever you've done to change his tonic has worked wonders."

Jameson was her black cat. I know, I know, what a stereotype. Then again, black cats need good homes, too. Jameson had kidney problems, and the apothecary had been giving him a weekly potion. I made the same potion for him that Trina had, but mine was working better for him.

"What can I do for you?" I asked.

A look of sadness crossed her face for a moment, but vanished. "I have to go on a trip sometime soon and I wanted to ask you to watch over Jameson.

"Of course," I said. He and I got along well and he didn't even mind moving over to my apartment the other times I'd taken care of him. "Going anyplace fun?"

"Not this time, I'm afraid. I've got family business to deal with and it can't be sorted out over the phone."

"No problem. Just say the word and I'll be there. How long do you think you'll be gone?"

She sighed. "Several days, so make sure you take the food and kitty litter with you."

She grabbed my hand and squeezed it. "You know there's no one I trust more with Jameson than you, right?"

I smiled. "That's very kind of you to say. I think he likes me, too."

She let go of my hand and forced a weak smile on her face. "Good. I'm glad the two of you get along so well."

I wanted to know why she looked sad. "Stay for some tea. I've got pomegranate oolong, but I can make anything else you want."

"No, thank you dear. I've got other errands to run before I leave town. And when I get back, you and I need to have a long talk."

I had no idea what she was talking about. "Sure. About what?"

She frowned. "Your future."

It's never good if someone frowns when they mention your future. She walked out into the sunshine and a sense of dread washed over me. This trip would not be good for her.

No sooner had the door closed than Caroline Arneson marched in.

"Good morning. How can I help you today?" I asked. There was no sense in assuming she was here to bully me out of my lease.

She lowered her sunglasses to reveal a black eye. Well, I say black, but it was more yellow-green, meaning it was a few days old and healing up. When I thought she had killed my mentor, Trina, Caroline confided in me that she knew how to handle her husband's anger. It didn't look like she succeeded a couple days ago.

"Are you okay?" I asked.

"Of course I am. I just need something to speed up the healing."

I bit my lip. I'd been gathering resources for abused women for months now, hoping I'd have an opportunity to give them to her. "I can help with that. But can we talk in my office first?"

She smiled. "Are you ready to move this failing business so I can take over your lease?"

"No. I just have something for you."

She followed me into my office and sat. I opened one of my desk drawers and pulled out a folder. "I worry about you, since you told me about your husband." I handed her the folder.

She opened it and scoffed. "This isn't for me. I can handle him."

She tossed the folder onto my desk.

"Are you sure about that? Your eye seems to tell a different story."

She stood up. "You're just a kid, what do you know? Now, do you have anything for me or not?"

"Yes. I've got a nice mixture of aloe, arnica, and bromelain that should do the trick. It's back out in the shop."

I followed her out of the office.

"Looks like you've bounced back from the robbery. It looks good in here," she said.

I handed her a small bottle of a bruise fading tincture. "Thanks. It's been a lot of work, but I think I'm doing well."

Leaf of Faith

"How much do I owe you?"

I blew my breath out. "Nothing, if you stop asking me to leave the building."

Her lips quirked into a small smile. "Guess I'd better pay you, then."

"Eleven dollars," I said.

As she fished through her bag for money, I stared at her, allowing my intuition to see if she needed anything else. Of course! The ingredients for Harmony Wash filled my vision: red rose petals, African violets, clover, crocus, elecampane, lemon verbena, and cinnamon. "I have one more thing for you."

"For the bruise?"

"No. It's just for...relaxation. It's a floral bubble bath. You look like you could use it." I wasn't really lying to her. It was a floral bubble bath, but if I told her it would bring harmony to her home, she'd laugh at me and not use it. "It's right over here."

I grabbed the bruise fader and led her to the display of bubble baths I'd created over the last month. "It's a new line of product I've created."

I held out a bottle to her. "On the house."

She handed me eleven dollars and took both bottles from my hands. "Thanks, kid."

What in Carnation is available for preorder NOW

Looking for more by Lisa Bouchard?

Join my mailing list at LisaBouchard.com for
a free prequel novella!

About the Author

It all started when she learned to read at five. One of her first and favorite memories is of words taped to all the objects in the house. Not long after that, books became the best thing ever and there was no turning back.

She suffered a crisis of confidence in High School and College and decided writing was too difficult, so she earned a degree in Chemistry and later enrolled in a Physics PhD program instead. Three career changes and four children later, she's back to writing and much happier for it.

Now she works from her home office in New Hampshire amid the books, kids, and occasional pets. Visit her at http://LisaBouchard.com.